"THE YELLOW WALLPAPER" AND "WHAT DIANTHA DID"

"THE YELLOW WALLPAPER" AND "WHAT DIANTHA DID"

CHARLOTTE PERKINS GILMAN

BROWNSTONE BOOKS

A BROWNSTONE BOOK

Published by Wildside Press, LLC
www.wildsidebooks.com

CONTENTS

INTRODUCTION: WHY I WROTE "THE YELLOW WALLPAPER"

Many and many a reader has asked that. When the story first came out, in the *New England Magazine* about 1891, a Boston physician made protest in *The Transcript*. Such a story ought not to be written, he said; it was enough to drive anyone mad to read it.

Another physician, in Kansas I think, wrote to say that it was the best description of incipient insanity he had ever seen, and—begging my pardon—had I been there?

Now the story of the story is this:

For many years I suffered from a severe and continuous nervous breakdown tending to melancholia—and beyond. During about the third year of this trouble I went, in devout faith and some faint stir of hope, to a noted specialist in nervous diseases, the best known in the country. This wise man put me to bed and applied the rest cure, to which a still-good physique responded so promptly that he concluded there was nothing much the matter with me, and sent me home with solemn advice to "live as domestic a life as far as possible," to "have but two hours' intellectual life a day," and "never to touch pen, brush, or pencil again" as long as I lived. This was in 1887.

I went home and obeyed those directions for some three months, and came so near the borderline of utter mental ruin that I could see over.

Then, using the remnants of intelligence that remained, and helped by a wise friend, I cast the noted specialist's advice to the winds and went to work again—work, the normal life of every human being; work, in which is joy and growth and service, without which one is a pauper and a parasite—ultimately recovering some measure of power.

Being naturally moved to rejoicing by this narrow escape, I wrote "The Yellow Wallpaper," with its embellishments and additions, to carry out the ideal (I never had hallucinations or objections to my mural decorations) and sent a copy to the physician who so nearly drove me mad. He never acknowledged it.

The little book is valued by alienists and as a good specimen of one kind of literature. It has, to my knowledge, saved one woman from a similar fate—so terrifying her family that they let her out into normal activity and she recovered.

But the best result is this. Many years later I was told that the great specialist had admitted to friends of his that he had altered his treatment of neurasthenia since reading "The Yellow Wallpaper."

It was not intended to drive people crazy, but to save people from being driven crazy, and it worked.

—Charlotte Perkins Gilman

THE YELLOW WALLPAPER

It is very seldom that mere ordinary people like John and myself secure ancestral halls for the summer.

A colonial mansion, a hereditary estate, I would say a haunted house, and reach the height of romantic felicity—but that would be asking too much of fate!

Still I will proudly declare that there is something queer about it.

Else, why should it be let so cheaply? And why have stood so long untenanted?

John laughs at me, of course, but one expects that in marriage.

John is practical in the extreme. He has no patience with faith, an intense horror of superstition, and he scoffs openly at any talk of things not to be felt and seen and put down in figures.

John is a physician, and *perhaps*—(I would not say it to a living soul, of course, but this is dead paper and a great relief to my mind)—*perhaps* that is one reason I do not get well faster.

You see he does not believe I am sick!

And what can one do?

If a physician of high standing, and one's own husband, assures friends and relatives that there is really nothing the matter with one but temporary nervous depression—a slight hysterical tendency—what is one to do?

My brother is also a physician, and also of high standing, and he says the same thing.

So I take phosphates or phosphites—whichever it is, and tonics, and journeys, and air, and exercise, and am absolutely forbidden to "work" until I am well again.

Personally, I disagree with their ideas.

Personally, I believe that congenial work, with excitement and change, would do me good.

But what is one to do?

I did write for a while in spite of them; but it *does* exhaust me a good deal—having to be so sly about it, or else meet with heavy opposition.

I sometimes fancy that in my condition if I had less opposition and more society and stimulus—but John says the very worst thing I can do is to think about my condition, and I confess it always makes me feel bad.

So I will let it alone and talk about the house.

The most beautiful place! It is quite alone, standing well back from the road, quite three miles from the village. It makes me think of English places that you read about, for there are hedges and walls and gates that lock, and lots of separate little houses for the gardeners and people.

There is a *delicious* garden! I never saw such a garden—large and shady, full of box-bordered paths, and lined with long grape-covered arbors with seats under them.

There were greenhouses, too, but they are all broken now.

There was some legal trouble, I believe, something about the heirs and coheirs; anyhow, the place has been empty for years.

That spoils my ghostliness, I am afraid, but I don't care—there is something strange about the house—I can feel it.

I even said so to John one moonlight evening, but he said what I felt was a DRAUGHT, and shut the window.

I get unreasonably angry with John sometimes. I'm sure I never used to be so sensitive. I think it is due to this nervous condition.

But John says if I feel so, I shall neglect proper self-control; so I take pains to control myself—before him, at least, and that makes me very tired.

I don't like our room a bit. I wanted one downstairs that opened on the piazza and had roses all over the window, and such pretty old-fashioned chintz hangings! but John would not hear of it.

He said there was only one window and not room for two beds, and no near room for him if he took another.

He is very careful and loving, and hardly lets me stir without special direction.

I have a schedule prescription for each hour in the day; he takes all care from me, and so I feel basely ungrateful not to value it more.

He said we came here solely on my account, that I was to have perfect rest and all the air I could get. "Your exercise depends on your strength, my dear," said he, "and your food somewhat on your appetite; but air you can absorb all the time." So we took the nursery at the top of the house.

It is a big, airy room, the whole floor nearly, with windows that look all ways, and air and sunshine galore. It was nursery first and then playroom and gymnasium, I should judge; for the windows are barred for little children, and there are rings and things in the walls.

The paint and paper look as if a boys' school had used it. It is stripped off—the paper—in great patches all around the head of my bed, about as far as I can reach, and in a great place on the other side of the room low down. I never saw a worse paper in my life.

One of those sprawling flamboyant patterns committing every artistic sin.

It is dull enough to confuse the eye in following, pronounced enough to constantly irritate and provoke study, and when you follow the lame uncertain curves for a little distance they suddenly commit suicide—plunge off at outrageous angles, destroy themselves in unheard of contradictions.

The color is repellent, almost revolting; a smouldering unclean yellow, strangely faded by the slow-turning sunlight.

It is a dull yet lurid orange in some places, a sickly sulphur tint in others.

No wonder the children hated it! I should hate it myself if I had to live in this room long.

There comes John, and I must put this away,—he hates to have me write a word.

We have been here two weeks, and I haven't felt like writing before, since that first day.

I am sitting by the window now, up in this atrocious nursery, and there is nothing to hinder my writing as much as I please, save lack of strength.

John is away all day, and even some nights when his cases are serious.

I am glad my case is not serious!

But these nervous troubles are dreadfully depressing.

John does not know how much I really suffer. He knows there is no *reason* to suffer, and that satisfies him.

Of course it is only nervousness. It does weigh on me so not to do my duty in any way!

I meant to be such a help to John, such a real rest and comfort, and here I am a comparative burden already!

Nobody would believe what an effort it is to do what little I am able,—to dress and entertain, and order things.

It is fortunate Mary is so good with the baby. Such a dear baby!

And yet I *cannot* be with him, it makes me so nervous.

I suppose John never was nervous in his life. He laughs at me so about this wall-paper!

At first he meant to repaper the room, but afterwards he said that I was letting it get the better of me, and that nothing was worse for a nervous patient than to give way to such fancies.

He said that after the wall-paper was changed it would be the heavy bedstead, and then the barred windows, and then that gate at the head of the stairs, and so on.

"You know the place is doing you good," he said, "and really, dear, I don't care to renovate the house just for a three months' rental."

"Then do let us go downstairs," I said, "there are such pretty rooms there."

Then he took me in his arms and called me a blessed little goose, and said he would go down to the cellar, if I wished, and have it whitewashed into the bargain.

But he is right enough about the beds and windows and things.

It is an airy and comfortable room as any one need wish, and, of course, I would not be so silly as to make him uncomfortable just for a whim.

I'm really getting quite fond of the big room, all but that horrid paper.

Out of one window I can see the garden, those mysterious deepshaded arbors, the riotous old-fashioned flowers, and bushes and gnarly trees.

Out of another I get a lovely view of the bay and a little private wharf belonging to the estate. There is a beautiful shaded lane that runs down there from the house. I always fancy I see people walking in these numerous paths and arbors, but John has cautioned me not to give way to fancy in the least. He says that with my imaginative power and habit of story-making, a nervous weakness like mine is sure to lead to all manner of excited fancies, and that I ought to use my will and good sense to check the tendency. So I try.

I think sometimes that if I were only well enough to write a little it would relieve the press of ideas and rest me.

But I find I get pretty tired when I try.

It is so discouraging not to have any advice and companionship about my work. When I get really well, John says we will ask Cousin Henry and Julia down for a long visit; but he says he would as soon put fireworks in my pillow-case as to let me have those stimulating people about now.

I wish I could get well faster.

But I must not think about that. This paper looks to me as if it *knew* what a vicious influence it had!

There is a recurrent spot where the pattern lolls like a broken neck and two bulbous eyes stare at you upside down.

I get positively angry with the impertinence of it and the everlastingness. Up and down and sideways they crawl, and those absurd, unblinking eyes are everywhere. There is one place where two breadths didn't match, and the eyes go all up and down the line, one a little higher than the other.

I never saw so much expression in an inanimate thing before, and we all know how much expression they have! I used to lie awake as a child and get more entertainment and terror out of blank walls and plain furniture than most children could find in a toy store.

I remember what a kindly wink the knobs of our big, old bureau used to have, and there was one chair that always seemed like a strong friend.

I used to feel that if any of the other things looked too fierce I could always hop into that chair and be safe.

The furniture in this room is no worse than inharmonious, however, for we had to bring it all from downstairs. I suppose when this was used as a playroom they had to take the nursery things out, and no wonder! I never saw such ravages as the children have made here.

The wall-paper, as I said before, is torn off in spots, and it sticketh closer than a brother—they must have had perseverance as well as hatred.

Then the floor is scratched and gouged and splintered, the plaster itself is dug out here and there, and this great heavy bed which is all we found in the room, looks as if it had been through the wars.

But I don't mind it a bit—only the paper.

There comes John's sister. Such a dear girl as she is, and so careful of me! I must not let her find me writing.

She is a perfect and enthusiastic housekeeper, and hopes for no better profession. I verily believe she thinks it is the writing which made me sick!

But I can write when she is out, and see her a long way off from these windows.

There is one that commands the road, a lovely shaded winding road, and one that just looks off over the country. A lovely country, too, full of great elms and velvet meadows.

This wall-paper has a kind of sub-pattern in a different shade, a particularly irritating one, for you can only see it in certain lights, and not clearly then.

But in the places where it isn't faded and where the sun is just so—I can see a strange, provoking, formless sort of figure, that seems to skulk about behind that silly and conspicuous front design.

There's sister on the stairs!

Well, the Fourth of July is over! The people are gone and I am tired out. John thought it might do me good to see a little company, so we just had mother and Nellie and the children down for a week.

Of course I didn't do a thing. Jennie sees to everything now.

But it tired me all the same.

John says if I don't pick up faster he shall send me to Weir Mitchell in the fall.

But I don't want to go there at all. I had a friend who was in his hands once, and she says he is just like John and my brother, only more so!

Besides, it is such an undertaking to go so far.

I don't feel as if it was worth while to turn my hand over for anything, and I'm getting dreadfully fretful and querulous.

I cry at nothing, and cry most of the time.

Of course I don't when John is here, or anybody else, but when I am alone.

And I am alone a good deal just now. John is kept in town very often by serious cases, and Jennie is good and lets me alone when I want her to.

So I walk a little in the garden or down that lovely lane, sit on the porch under the roses, and lie down up here a good deal.

I'm getting really fond of the room in spite of the wall-paper. Perhaps *because* of the wall-paper.

It dwells in my mind so!

I lie here on this great immovable bed—it is nailed down, I believe—and follow that pattern about by the hour. It is as good as gymnastics, I assure you. I start, we'll say, at the bottom, down in the corner over there where it has not been touched, and I determine for the thousandth time that I WILL follow that pointless pattern to some sort of a conclusion.

I know a little of the principle of design, and I know this thing was not arranged on any laws of radiation, or alternation, or repetition, or symmetry, or anything else that I ever heard of.

It is repeated, of course, by the breadths, but not otherwise.

Looked at in one way each breadth stands alone, the bloated curves and flourishes—a kind of "debased Romanesque" with delirium tremens—go waddling up and down in isolated columns of fatuity.

But, on the other hand, they connect diagonally, and the sprawling outlines run off in great slanting waves of optic horror, like a lot of wallowing seaweeds in full chase.

The whole thing goes horizontally, too, at least it seems so, and I exhaust myself in trying to distinguish the order of its going in that direction.

They have used a horizontal breadth for a frieze, and that adds wonderfully to the confusion.

There is one end of the room where it is almost intact, and there, when the crosslights fade and the low sun shines directly upon it, I can almost fancy radiation after all,—the interminable grotesques seem to form around a common centre and rush off in headlong plunges of equal distraction.

It makes me tired to follow it. I will take a nap I guess.

I don't know why I should write this.

I don't want to.

I don't feel able.

And I know John would think it absurd. But I MUST say what I feel and think in some way—it is such a relief!

But the effort is getting to be greater than the relief.

Half the time now I am awfully lazy, and lie down ever so much.

John says I musn't lose my strength, and has me take cod liver oil and lots of tonics and things, to say nothing of ale and wine and rare meat.

Dear John! He loves me very dearly, and hates to have me sick. I tried to have a real earnest reasonable talk with him the other day, and tell him how I wish he would let me go and make a visit to Cousin Henry and Julia.

But he said I wasn't able to go, nor able to stand it after I got there; and I did not make out a very good case for myself, for I was crying before I had finished.

It is getting to be a great effort for me to think straight. Just this nervous weakness I suppose.

And dear John gathered me up in his arms, and just carried me upstairs and laid me on the bed, and sat by me and read to me till it tired my head.

He said I was his darling and his comfort and all he had, and that I must take care of myself for his sake, and keep well.

He says no one but myself can help me out of it, that I must use my will and self-control and not let any silly fancies run away with me.

There's one comfort, the baby is well and happy, and does not have to occupy this nursery with the horrid wall-paper.

If we had not used it, that blessed child would have! What a fortunate escape! Why, I wouldn't have a child of mine, an impressionable little thing, live in such a room for worlds.

I never thought of it before, but it is lucky that John kept me here after all, I can stand it so much easier than a baby, you see.

Of course I never mention it to them any more—I am too wise,—but I keep watch of it all the same.

There are things in that paper that nobody knows but me, or ever will.

Behind that outside pattern the dim shapes get clearer every day.

It is always the same shape, only very numerous.

And it is like a woman stooping down and creeping about behind that pattern. I don't like it a bit. I wonder—I begin to think—I wish John would take me away from here!

It is so hard to talk with John about my case, because he is so wise, and because he loves me so.

But I tried it last night.

It was moonlight. The moon shines in all around just as the sun does.

I hate to see it sometimes, it creeps so slowly, and always comes in by one window or another.

John was asleep and I hated to waken him, so I kept still and watched the moonlight on that undulating wall-paper till I felt creepy.

The faint figure behind seemed to shake the pattern, just as if she wanted to get out.

I got up softly and went to feel and see if the paper *did* move, and when I came back John was awake.

"What is it, little girl?" he said. "Don't go walking about like that—you'll get cold."

I though it was a good time to talk, so I told him that I really was not gaining here, and that I wished he would take me away.

"Why darling!" said he, "our lease will be up in three weeks, and I can't see how to leave before.

"The repairs are not done at home, and I cannot possibly leave town just now. Of course if you were in any danger, I could and would, but you really are better, dear, whether you can see it or not. I am a doctor, dear, and I know. You are gaining flesh and color, your appetite is better, I feel really much easier about you."

"I don't weigh a bit more," said I, "nor as much; and my appetite may be better in the evening when you are here, but it is worse in the morning when you are away!"

"Bless her little heart!" said he with a big hug, "she shall be as sick as she pleases! But now let's improve the shining hours by going to sleep, and talk about it in the morning!"

"And you won't go away?" I asked gloomily.

"Why, how can I, dear? It is only three weeks more and then we will take a nice little trip of a few days while Jennie is getting the house ready. Really dear you are better!"

"Better in body perhaps—" I began, and stopped short, for he sat up straight and looked at me with such a stern, reproachful look that I could not say another word.

"My darling," said he, "I beg of you, for my sake and for our child's sake, as well as for your own, that you will never for one instant let that idea enter your mind! There is nothing so dangerous, so fascinating, to a temperament like yours. It is a false and foolish fancy. Can you not trust me as a physician when I tell you so?"

So of course I said no more on that score, and we went to sleep before long. He thought I was asleep first, but I wasn't, and lay there for hours trying to decide whether that front pattern and the back pattern really did move together or separately.

On a pattern like this, by daylight, there is a lack of sequence, a defiance of law, that is a constant irritant to a normal mind.

The color is hideous enough, and unreliable enough, and infuriating enough, but the pattern is torturing.

You think you have mastered it, but just as you get well underway in following, it turns a back-somersault and there you are. It slaps you in the face, knocks you down, and tramples upon you. It is like a bad dream.

The outside pattern is a florid arabesque, reminding one of a fungus. If you can imagine a toadstool in joints, an interminable string of toadstools, budding and sprouting in endless convolutions—why, that is something like it.

That is, sometimes!

There is one marked peculiarity about this paper, a thing nobody seems to notice but myself, and that is that it changes as the light changes.

When the sun shoots in through the east window—I always watch for that first long, straight ray—it changes so quickly that I never can quite believe it.

That is why I watch it always.

By moonlight—the moon shines in all night when there is a moon—I wouldn't know it was the same paper.

At night in any kind of light, in twilight, candle light, lamp-light, and worst of all by moonlight, it becomes bars! The outside pattern I mean, and the woman behind it is as plain as can be.

I didn't realize for a long time what the thing was that showed behind, that dim sub-pattern, but now I am quite sure it is a woman.

By daylight she is subdued, quiet. I fancy it is the pattern that keeps her so still. It is so puzzling. It keeps me quiet by the hour.

I lie down ever so much now. John says it is good for me, and to sleep all I can.

Indeed he started the habit by making me lie down for an hour after each meal.

It is a very bad habit I am convinced, for you see I don't sleep.

And that cultivates deceit, for I don't tell them I'm awake—O no!

The fact is I am getting a little afraid of John.

He seems very queer sometimes, and even Jennie has an inexplicable look.

It strikes me occasionally, just as a scientific hypothesis,—that perhaps it is the paper!

I have watched John when he did not know I was looking, and come into the room suddenly on the most innocent excuses, and I've caught him several times *looking at the paper*! And Jennie too. I caught Jennie with her hand on it once.

She didn't know I was in the room, and when I asked her in a quiet, a very quiet voice, with the most restrained manner possible, what she was doing with the paper—she turned around as if she had been caught stealing, and looked quite angry—asked me why I should frighten her so!

Then she said that the paper stained everything it touched, that she had found yellow smooches on all my clothes and John's, and she wished we would be more careful!

Did not that sound innocent? But I know she was studying that pattern, and I am determined that nobody shall find it out but myself!

Life is very much more exciting now than it used to be. You see I have something more to expect, to look forward to, to watch. I really do eat better, and am more quiet than I was.

John is so pleased to see me improve! He laughed a little the other day, and said I seemed to be flourishing in spite of my wall-paper.

I turned it off with a laugh. I had no intention of telling him it was *because* of the wall-paper—he would make fun of me. He might even want to take me away.

I don't want to leave now until I have found it out. There is a week more, and I think that will be enough.

I'm feeling ever so much better! I don't sleep much at night, for it is so interesting to watch developments; but I sleep a good deal in the daytime.

In the daytime it is tiresome and perplexing.

There are always new shoots on the fungus, and new shades of yellow all over it. I cannot keep count of them, though I have tried conscientiously.

It is the strangest yellow, that wall-paper! It makes me think of all the yellow things I ever saw—not beautiful ones like buttercups, but old foul, bad yellow things.

But there is something else about that paper—the smell! I noticed it the moment we came into the room, but with so much air and sun it was not bad. Now we have had a week of fog and rain, and whether the windows are open or not, the smell is here.

It creeps all over the house.

I find it hovering in the dining-room, skulking in the parlor, hiding in the hall, lying in wait for me on the stairs.

It gets into my hair.

Even when I go to ride, if I turn my head suddenly and surprise it—there is that smell!

Such a peculiar odor, too! I have spent hours in trying to analyze it, to find what it smelled like.

It is not bad—at first, and very gentle, but quite the subtlest, most enduring odor I ever met.

In this damp weather it is awful, I wake up in the night and find it hanging over me.

It used to disturb me at first. I thought seriously of burning the house—to reach the smell.

But now I am used to it. The only thing I can think of that it is like is the *color* of the paper! A yellow smell.

There is a very funny mark on this wall, low down, near the mopboard. A streak that runs round the room. It goes behind every piece of furniture, except the bed, a long, straight, even *smooch*, as if it had been rubbed over and over.

I wonder how it was done and who did it, and what they did it for. Round and round and round—round and round and round—it makes me dizzy!

I really have discovered something at last.

Through watching so much at night, when it changes so, I have finally found out.

The front pattern does move—and no wonder! The woman behind shakes it!

Sometimes I think there are a great many women behind, and sometimes only one, and she crawls around fast, and her crawling shakes it all over.

Then in the very bright spots she keeps still, and in the very shady spots she just takes hold of the bars and shakes them hard.

And she is all the time trying to climb through. But nobody could climb through that pattern—it strangles so; I think that is why it has so many heads.

They get through, and then the pattern strangles them off and turns them upside down, and makes their eyes white!

If those heads were covered or taken off it would not be half so bad.

I think that woman gets out in the daytime!

And I'll tell you why—privately—I've seen her!

I can see her out of every one of my windows!

It is the same woman, I know, for she is always creeping, and most women do not creep by daylight.

I see her on that long road under the trees, creeping along, and when a carriage comes she hides under the blackberry vines.

I don't blame her a bit. It must be very humiliating to be caught creeping by daylight!

I always lock the door when I creep by daylight. I can't do it at night, for I know John would suspect something at once.

And John is so queer now, that I don't want to irritate him. I wish he would take another room! Besides, I don't want anybody to get that woman out at night but myself.

I often wonder if I could see her out of all the windows at once.

But, turn as fast as I can, I can only see out of one at one time.

And though I always see her, she *may* be able to creep faster than I can turn!

I have watched her sometimes away off in the open country, creeping as fast as a cloud shadow in a high wind.

If only that top pattern could be gotten off from the under one! I mean to try it, little by little.

I have found out another funny thing, but I shan't tell it this time! It does not do to trust people too much.

There are only two more days to get this paper off, and I believe John is beginning to notice. I don't like the look in his eyes.

And I heard him ask Jennie a lot of professional questions about me. She had a very good report to give.

She said I slept a good deal in the daytime.

John knows I don't sleep very well at night, for all I'm so quiet!

He asked me all sorts of questions, too, and pretended to be very loving and kind.

As if I couldn't see through him!

Still, I don't wonder he acts so, sleeping under this paper for three months.

It only interests me, but I feel sure John and Jennie are secretly affected by it.

Hurrah! This is the last day, but it is enough. John is to stay in town over night, and won't be out until this evening.

Jennie wanted to sleep with me—the sly thing! but I told her I should undoubtedly rest better for a night all alone.

That was clever, for really I wasn't alone a bit! As soon as it was moonlight and that poor thing began to crawl and shake the pattern, I got up and ran to help her.

I pulled and she shook, I shook and she pulled, and before morning we had peeled off yards of that paper.

A strip about as high as my head and half around the room.

And then when the sun came and that awful pattern began to

laugh at me, I declared I would finish it to-day!

We go away to-morrow, and they are moving all my furniture down again to leave things as they were before.

Jennie looked at the wall in amazement, but I told her merrily that I did it out of pure spite at the vicious thing.

She laughed and said she wouldn't mind doing it herself, but I must not get tired.

How she betrayed herself that time!

But I am here, and no person touches this paper but me—not *alive*!

She tried to get me out of the room—it was too patent! But I said it was so quiet and empty and clean now that I believed I would lie down again and sleep all I could; and not to wake me even for dinner—I would call when I woke.

So now she is gone, and the servants are gone, and the things are gone, and there is nothing left but that great bedstead nailed down, with the canvas mattress we found on it.

We shall sleep downstairs to-night, and take the boat home to-morrow.

I quite enjoy the room, now it is bare again.

How those children did tear about here!

This bedstead is fairly gnawed!

But I must get to work.

I have locked the door and thrown the key down into the front path.

I don't want to go out, and I don't want to have anybody come in, till John comes.

I want to astonish him.

I've got a rope up here that even Jennie did not find. If that woman does get out, and tries to get away, I can tie her!

But I forgot I could not reach far without anything to stand on!

This bed will *not* move!

I tried to lift and push it until I was lame, and then I got so angry I bit off a little piece at one corner—but it hurt my teeth.

Then I peeled off all the paper I could reach standing on the floor. It sticks horribly and the pattern just enjoys it! All those strangled heads and bulbous eyes and waddling fungus growths just shriek with derision!

I am getting angry enough to do something desperate. To jump out of the window would be admirable exercise, but the bars are too strong even to try.

Besides I wouldn't do it. Of course not. I know well enough that a step like that is improper and might be misconstrued.

I don't like to *look* out of the windows even—there are so many of those creeping women, and they creep so fast.

I wonder if they all come out of that wall-paper as I did?

But I am securely fastened now by my well-hidden rope—you don't get ME out in the road there!

I suppose I shall have to get back behind the pattern when it comes night, and that is hard!

It is so pleasant to be out in this great room and creep around as I please!

I don't want to go outside. I won't, even if Jennie asks me to.

For outside you have to creep on the ground, and everything is green instead of yellow.

But here I can creep smoothly on the floor, and my shoulder just fits in that long smooch around the wall, so I cannot lose my way.

Why there's John at the door!

It is no use, young man, you can't open it!

How he does call and pound!

Now he's crying for an axe.

It would be a shame to break down that beautiful door!

"John dear!" said I in the gentlest voice, "the key is down by the front steps, under a plantain leaf!"

That silenced him for a few moments.

Then he said—very quietly indeed, "Open the door, my darling!"

"I can't," said I. "The key is down by the front door under a plantain leaf!"

And then I said it again, several times, very gently and slowly, and said it so often that he had to go and see, and he got it of course, and came in. He stopped short by the door.

"What is the matter?" he cried. "For God's sake, what are you doing!"

I kept on creeping just the same, but I looked at him over my shoulder.

"I've got out at last," said I, "in spite of you and Jane. And I've pulled off most of the paper, so you can't put me back!"

Now why should that man have fainted? But he did, and right across my path by the wall, so that I had to creep over him every time!

WHAT DIANTHA DID

CHAPTER I: HANDICAPPED

One may use the Old Man of the Sea,
For a partner or patron,
But helpless and hapless is he
Who is ridden, inextricably,
By a fond old mer-matron.

The Warden house was more impressive in appearance than its neighbors. It had "grounds," instead of a yard or garden; it had wide pillared porches and "galleries," showing southern antecedents; moreover, it had a cupola, giving date to the building, and proof of the continuing ambitions of the builders.

The stately mansion was covered with heavy flowering vines, also with heavy mortgages. Mrs. Roscoe Warden and her four daughters reposed peacefully under the vines, while Roscoe Warden, Jr., struggled desperately under the mortgages.

A slender, languid lady was Mrs. Warden, wearing her thin but still brown hair in "water-waves" over a pale high forehead. She was sitting on a couch on the broad, rose-shaded porch, surrounded by billowing masses of vari-colored worsted. It was her delight to purchase skein on skein of soft, bright-hued wool, cut it all up into short lengths, tie them together again in contrasting colors, and then crochet this hashed rainbow into afghans of startling aspect. California does not call for afghans to any great extent, but "they make such acceptable presents," Mrs. Warden declared, to those who questioned the purpose of her work; and she continued to send them off, on Christmases, birthdays, and minor weddings, in a stream of pillowy bundles. As they were accepted, they must have been acceptable, and the stream flowed on.

Around her, among the gay blossoms and gayer wools, sat

her four daughters, variously intent. The mother, a poetic soul, had named them musically and with dulcet rhymes: Madeline and Adeline were the two eldest, Coraline and Doraline the two youngest. It had not occurred to her until too late that those melodious terminations made it impossible to call one daughter without calling two, and that "Lina" called them all.

"Mis' Immerjin," said a soft voice in the doorway, "dere pos'tively ain't no butter in de house fer supper."

"No butter?" said Mrs. Warden, incredulously. "Why, Sukey, I'm sure we had a tub sent up last—last Tuesday!"

"A week ago Tuesday, more likely, mother," suggested Dora.

"Nonsense, Dora! It was this week, wasn't it, girls?" The mother appealed to them quite earnestly, as if the date of that tub's delivery would furnish forth the supper-table; but none of the young ladies save Dora had even a contradiction to offer.

"You know I never notice things," said the artistic Cora; and "the de-lines," as their younger sisters called them, said nothing.

"I might borrow some o' Mis' Bell?" suggested Sukey; "dat's nearer 'n' de sto'."

"Yes, do, Sukey," her mistress agreed. "It is so hot. But what have you done with that tubful?"

"Why, some I tuk back to Mis' Bell for what I borrered befo'—I'm always most careful to make return for what I borrers—and yo' know, Mis' Warden, dat waffles and sweet potaters and cohn bread dey do take butter; to say nothin' o' them little cakes you all likes so well—*an'* de fried chicken, *an'*—"

"Never mind, Sukey; you go and present my compliments to Mrs. Bell, and ask her for some; and be sure you return it promptly. Now, girls, don't let me forget to tell Ross to send up another tub."

"We can't seem to remember any better than you can, mother," said Adeline, dreamily. "Those details are so utterly uninteresting."

"I should think it was Sukey's business to tell him," said

Madeline with decision; while the "a-lines" kept silence this time.

"There! Sukey's gone!" Mrs. Warden suddenly remarked, watching the stout figure moving heavily away under the pepper trees. "And I meant to have asked her to make me a glass of shrub! Dora, dear, you run and get it for mother."

Dora laid down her work, not too regretfully, and started off.

"That child is the most practical of any of you," said her mother; which statement was tacitly accepted. It was not extravagant praise.

Dora poked about in the refrigerator for a bit of ice. She had no idea of the high cost of ice in that region—it came from "the store," like all their provisions. It did not occur to her that fish and milk and melons made a poor combination in flavor; or that the clammy, sub-offensive smell was not the natural and necessary odor of refrigerators. Neither did she think that a sunny corner of the back porch near the chimney, though convenient, was an ill-selected spot for a refrigerator. She couldn't find the ice-pick, so put a big piece of ice in a towel and broke it on the edge of the sink; replaced the largest fragment, used what she wanted, and left the rest to filter slowly down through a mass of grease and tea-leaves; found the raspberry vinegar, and made a very satisfactory beverage which her mother received with grateful affection.

"Thank you, my darling," she said. "I wish you'd made a pitcherful."

"Why didn't you, Do?" her sisters demanded.

"You're too late," said Dora, hunting for her needle and then for her thimble, and then for her twist; "but there's more in the kitchen."

"I'd rather go without than go into the kitchen," said Adeline; "I do despise a kitchen." And this seemed to be the general sentiment; for no one moved.

"My mother always liked raspberry shrub," said Mrs. Warden; "and your Aunt Leicester, and your Raymond cousins."

Mrs. Warden had a wide family circle, many beloved relatives, "connections" of whom she was duly proud and "kin" in such widening ramifications that even her carefully reared daughters lost track of them.

"You young people don't seem to care about your cousins at all!" pursued their mother, somewhat severely, setting her glass on the railing, from whence it was presently knocked off and broken.

"That's the fifth!" remarked Dora, under breath.

"Why should we, Ma?" inquired Cora. "We've never seen one of them—except Madam Weatherstone!"

"We'll never forget *her!*" said Madeline, with delicate decision, laying down the silk necktie she was knitting for Roscoe. "What *beautiful* manners she had!"

"How rich is she, mother? Do you know?" asked Dora.

"Rich enough to do something for Roscoe, I'm sure, if she had a proper family spirit," replied Mrs. Warden. "Her mother was own cousin to my grandmother—one of the Virginia Paddingtons. Or she might do something for you girls."

"I wish she would!" Adeline murmured, softly, her large eyes turned to the horizon, her hands in her lap over the handkerchief she was marking for Roscoe.

"Don't be ungrateful, Adeline," said her mother, firmly. "You have a good home and a good brother; no girl ever had a better."

"But there is never anything going on," broke in Coraline, in a tone of complaint; "no parties, no going away for vacations, no anything."

"Now, Cora, don't be discontented! You must not add a straw to dear Roscoe's burdens," said her mother.

"Of course not, mother; I wouldn't for the world. I never saw her but that once; and she wasn't very cordial. But, as you say, she might do *something*. She might invite us to visit her."

"If she ever comes back again, I'm going to recite for her," said, Dora, firmly.

Her mother gazed fondly on her youngest. "I wish you could, dear," she agreed. "I'm sure you have talent; and Madam Weatherstone would recognize it. And Adeline's music too.

And Cora's art. I am very proud of my girls."

Cora sat where the light fell well upon her work. She was illuminating a volume of poems, painting flowers on the margins, in appropriate places—for Roscoe.

"I wonder if he'll care for it?" she said, laying down her brush and holding the book at arm's length to get the effect.

"Of course he will!" answered her mother, warmly. "It is not only the beauty of it, but the affection! How are you getting on, Dora?"

Dora was laboring at a task almost beyond her fourteen years, consisting of a negligee shirt of outing flannel, upon the breast of which she was embroidering a large, intricate design—for Roscoe. She was an ambitious child, but apt to tire in the execution of her large projects.

"I guess it'll be done," she said, a little wearily. "What are you going to give him, mother?"

"Another bath-robe; his old one is so worn. And nothing is too good for my boy."

"He's coming," said Adeline, who was still looking down the road; and they all concealed their birthday work in haste.

A tall, straight young fellow, with an air of suddenly-faced maturity upon him, opened the gate under the pepper trees and came toward them.

He had the finely molded features we see in portraits of handsome ancestors, seeming to call for curling hair a little longish, and a rich profusion of ruffled shirt. But his hair was sternly short, his shirt severely plain, his proudly carried head spoke of effort rather than of ease in its attitude.

Dora skipped to meet him, Cora descended a decorous step or two. Madeline and Adeline, arm in arm, met him at the piazza edge, his mother lifted her face.

"Well, mother, dear!" Affectionately he stooped and kissed her, and she held his hand and stroked it lovingly. The sisters gathered about with teasing affection, Dora poking in his coat-pocket for the stick candy her father always used to bring her, and her brother still remembered.

"Aren't you home early, dear?" asked Mrs. Warden.

"Yes; I had a little headache"—he passed his hand over his forehead—"and Joe can run the store till after supper, anyhow." They flew to get him camphor, cologne, a menthol-pencil. Dora dragged forth the wicker lounge. He was laid out carefully and fanned and fussed over till his mother drove them all away.

"Now, just rest," she said. "It's an hour to supper time yet!" And she covered him with her latest completed afghan, gathering up and carrying away the incomplete one and its tumultuous constituents.

He was glad of the quiet, the fresh, sweet air, the smell of flowers instead of the smell of molasses and cheese, soap and sulphur matches. But the headache did not stop, nor the worry that caused it. He loved his mother, he loved his sisters, he loved their home, but he did not love the grocery business which had fallen so unexpectedly upon him at his father's death, nor the load of debt which fell with it.

That they need never have had so large a "place" to "keep up" did not occur to him. He had lived there most of his life, and it was home. That the expenses of running the household were three times what they needed to be, he did not know. His father had not questioned their style of living, nor did he. That a family of five women might, between them, do the work of the house, he did not even consider.

Mrs. Warden's health was never good, and since her husband's death she had made daily use of many afghans on the many lounges of the house. Madeline was "delicate," and Adeline was "frail"; Cora was "nervous," Dora was "only a child." So black Sukey and her husband Jonah did the work of the place, so far as it was done; and Mrs. Warden held it a miracle of management that she could "do with one servant," and the height of womanly devotion on her daughters' part that they dusted the parlor and arranged the flowers.

Roscoe shut his eyes and tried to rest, but his problem beset him ruthlessly. There was the store—their one and only source of income. There was the house, a steady, large expense. There were five women to clothe and keep contented, beside himself. There was the unappeasable demand of the mortgage—and there was Diantha.

When Mr. Warden died, some four years previously, Roscoe was a lad of about twenty, just home from college, full of dreams of great service to the world in science, expecting to go back for his doctor's degree next year. Instead of which the older man had suddenly dropped beneath the burden he had carried with such visible happiness and pride, such unknown anxiety and straining effort; and the younger one had to step into the harness on the spot.

He was brave, capable, wholly loyal to his mother and sisters, reared in the traditions of older days as to a man's duty toward women. In his first grief for his father, and the ready pride with which he undertook to fill his place, he had not in the least estimated the weight of care he was to carry, nor the time that he must carry it. A year, a year or two, a few years, he told himself, as they passed, and he would make more money; the girls, of course, would marry; he could "retire" in time and take up his scientific work again. Then—there was Diantha.

When he found he loved this young neighbor of theirs, and that she loved him, the first flush of happiness made all life look easier. They had been engaged six months—and it was beginning to dawn upon the young man that it might be six years—or sixteen years—before he could marry.

He could not sell the business—and if he could, he knew of no better way to take care of his family. The girls did not marry, and even when they did, he had figured this out to a dreary certainty, he would still not be free. To pay the mortgages off, and keep up the house, even without his sisters, would require all the money the store would bring in for some six years ahead. The young man set his teeth hard and turned his head sharply toward the road.

And there was Diantha.

She stood at the gate and smiled at him. He sprang to his feet, headacheless for the moment, and joined her. Mrs. Warden, from the lounge by her bedroom window, saw them move off together, and sighed.

"Poor Roscoe!" she said to herself. "It is very hard for him. But he carries his difficulties nobly. He is a son to be proud of." And she wept a little.

Diantha slipped her hand in his offered arm—he clasped it warmly with his, and they walked along together.

"You won't come in and see mother and the girls?"

"No, thank you; not this time. I must get home and get supper. Besides, I'd rather see just you."

He felt it a pity that there were so many houses along the road here, but squeezed her hand, anyhow.

She looked at him keenly. "Headache?" she asked.

"Yes; it's nothing; it's gone already."

"Worry?" she asked.

"Yes, I suppose it is," he answered. "But I ought not to worry. I've got a good home, a good mother, good sisters, and—you!" And he took advantage of a high hedge and an empty lot on either side of them.

Diantha returned his kiss affectionately enough, but seemed preoccupied, and walked in silence till he asked her what she was thinking about.

"About you, of course," she answered, brightly. "There are things I want to say; and yet—I ought not to."

"You can say anything on earth to me," he answered.

"You are twenty-four," she began, musingly.

"Admitted at once."

"And I'm twenty-one and a half."

"That's no such awful revelation, surely!"

"And we've been engaged ever since my birthday," the girl pursued.

"All these are facts, dearest."

"Now, Ross, will you be perfectly frank with me? May I ask you an—an impertinent question?"

"You may ask me any question you like; it couldn't be impertinent."

"You'll be scandalised, I know—but—well, here goes. What would you think if Madeline—or any of the girls—should go away to work?"

He looked at her lovingly, but with a little smile on his firm mouth.

"I shouldn't allow it," he said.

"O—allow it? I asked you what you'd think."

"I should think it was a disgrace to the family, and a direct reproach to me," he answered. "But it's no use talking about that. None of the girls have any such foolish notion. And I wouldn't permit it if they had."

Diantha smiled. "I suppose you never would permit your wife to work?"

"My widow might have to—not my wife." He held his fine head a trifle higher, and her hand ached for a moment.

"Wouldn't you let me work—to help you, Ross?"

"My dearest girl, you've got something far harder than that to do for me, and that's wait."

His face darkened again, and he passed his hand over his forehead. "Sometimes I feel as if I ought not to hold you at all!" he burst out, bitterly. "You ought to be free to marry a better man."

"There aren't any!" said Diantha, shaking her head slowly from side to side. "And if there were—millions—I wouldn't marry any of 'em. I love *you*," she firmly concluded.

"Then we'll just *wait*," said he, setting his teeth on the word, as if he would crush it. "It won't be hard with you to help. You're better worth it than Rachael and Leah together." They walked a few steps silently.

"But how about science?" she asked him.

"I don't let myself think of it. I'll take that up later. We're young enough, both of us, to wait for our happiness."

"And have you any idea—we might as well face the worst—how many years do you think that will be, dearest?"

He was a little annoyed at her persistence. Also, though he would not admit the thought, it did not seem quite the thing for her to ask. A woman should not seek too definite a period of waiting. She ought to trust—to just wait on general principles.

"I can face a thing better if I know just what I'm facing," said the girl, quietly, "and I'd wait for you, if I had to, all my life. Will it be twenty years, do you think?"

He looked relieved. "Why, no, indeed, darling. It oughtn't to be at the outside more than five. Or six," he added, honest though reluctant.

"You see, father had no time to settle anything; there were outstanding accounts, and the funeral expenses, and the mortgages. But the business is good; and I can carry it; I can build it up." He shook his broad shoulders determinedly. "I should think it might be within five, perhaps even less. Good things happen sometimes—such as you, my heart's delight."

They were at her gate now, and she stood a little while to say good-night. A step inside there was a seat, walled in by evergreen, roofed over by the wide acacia boughs. Many a long good-night had they exchanged there, under the large, brilliant California moon. They sat there, silent, now.

Diantha's heart was full of love for him, and pride and confidence in him; but it was full of other feelings, too, which he could not fathom. His trouble was clearer to her than to him; as heavy to bear. To her mind, trained in all the minutiae of domestic economy, the Warden family lived in careless wastefulness. That five women—for Dora was older than she had been when she began to do housework—should require servants, seemed to this New England-born girl mere laziness and pride. That two voting women over twenty should prefer being supported by their brother to supporting themselves, she condemned even more sharply. Moreover, she felt well assured that with a different family to "support," Mr. Warden would never have broken down so suddenly and irrecoverably. Even that funeral—her face hardened as she thought of the conspicuous "lot," the continual flowers, the monument (not wholly paid for yet, that monument, though this she did not know)—all that expenditure to do honor to the man they had worked to death (thus brutally Diantha put it) was probably enough to put off their happiness for a whole year.

She rose at last, her hand still held in his. "I'm sorry, but I've got to get supper, dear," she said, "and you must go. Good-night for the present; you'll be round by and by?"

"Yes, for a little while, after we close up," said he, and took himself off, not too suddenly, walking straight and proud while her eyes were on him, throwing her a kiss from the corner; but his step lagging and his headache settling down upon him again as he neared the large house with the cupola.

Diantha watched him out of sight, turned and marched up the path to her own door, her lips set tight, her well-shaped head as straightly held as his. "It's a shame, a cruel, burning shame!" she told herself rebelliously. "A man of his ability. Why, he could do anything, in his own work! And he loved it so!

"To keep a grocery store!!!!!

"And nothing to show for all that splendid effort!"

"They don't do a thing? They just *live*—and 'keep house!' All those women!

"Six years? Likely to be sixty! But I'm not going to wait!"

CHAPTER II: AN UNNATURAL DAUGHTER

The brooding bird fulfills her task,
 Or she-bear lean and brown;
All parent beasts see duty true,
All parent beasts their duty do,
We are the only kind that asks
 For duty upside down.

The stiff-rayed windmill stood like a tall mechanical flower, turning slowly in the light afternoon wind; its faint regular metallic squeak pricked the dry silence wearingly. Rampant fuchsias, red-jewelled, heavy, ran up its framework, with crowding heliotrope and nasturtiums. Thick straggling roses hung over the kitchen windows, and a row of dusty eucalyptus trees rustled their stiff leaves, and gave an ineffectual shade to the house.

It was one of those small frame houses common to the northeastern states, which must be dear to the hearts of their dwellers. For no other reason, surely, would the cold grey steep-roofed little boxes be repeated so faithfully in the broad glow of a semi-tropical landscape. There was an attempt at a "lawn," the pet ambition of the transplanted easterner; and a further attempt at "flower-beds," which merely served as a sort of springboard to their far-reaching products.

The parlor, behind the closed blinds, was as New England parlors are; minus the hint of cosiness given by even a fireless stove; the little bedrooms baked under the roof; only the kitchen spoke of human living, and the living it portrayed was not, to say the least, joyous. It was clean, clean with a cleanness that spoke of conscientious labor and unremitting care. The zinc mat under the big cook-stove was scoured to a dull glimmer, while that swart altar itself shone darkly from its daily rubbing.

There was no dust nor smell of dust; no grease spots, no litter anywhere. But the place bore no atmosphere of contented pride, as does a Dutch, German or French kitchen, it spoke of Labor, Economy and Duty—under restriction.

In the dead quiet of the afternoon Diantha and her mother sat there sewing. The sun poured down through the dangling eucalyptus leaves. The dry air, rich with flower odors, flowed softly in, pushing the white sash curtains a steady inch or two. Ee-errr!—Ee-errr!—came the faint whine of the windmill.

To the older woman rocking in her small splint chair by the rose-draped window, her thoughts dwelling on long dark green grass, the shade of elms, and cows knee-deep in river-shallows; this was California—hot, arid, tedious in endless sunlight—a place of exile.

To the younger, the long seam of the turned sheet pinned tightly to her knee, her needle flying firmly and steadily, and her thoughts full of pouring moonlight through acacia boughs and Ross's murmured words, it was California—rich, warm, full of sweet bloom and fruit, of boundless vitality, promise, and power—home!

Mrs. Bell drew a long weary sigh, and laid down her work for a moment.

"Why don't you stop it Mother dear? There's surely no hurry about these things."

"No—not particularly," her mother answered, "but there's plenty else to do." And she went on with the long neat hemming. Diantha did the "over and over seam" up the middle.

"What *do* you do it for anyway, Mother—I always hated this job—and you don't seem to like it."

"They wear almost twice as long, child, you know. The middle gets worn and the edges don't. Now they're reversed. As to liking it—" She gave a little smile, a smile that was too tired to be sarcastic, but which certainly did not indicate pleasure.

"What kind of work do you like best—really?" her daughter inquired suddenly, after a silent moment or two.

"Why—I don't know," said her mother. "I never thought of it. I never tried any but teaching. I didn't like that. Neither did your Aunt Esther, but she's still teaching."

"Didn't you like any of it?" pursued Diantha.

"I liked arithmetic best. I always loved arithmetic, when I went to school—used to stand highest in that."

"And what part of housework do you like best?" the girl persisted.

Mrs. Bell smiled again, wanly. "Seems to me sometimes as if I couldn't tell sometimes what part I like least!" she answered. Then with sudden heat—"O my Child! Don't you marry till Ross can afford at least one girl for you!"

Diantha put her small, strong hands behind her head and leaned back in her chair. "We'll have to wait some time for that I fancy," she said. "But, Mother, there is one part you like—keeping accounts! I never saw anything like the way you manage the money, and I believe you've got every bill since you were married."

"Yes—I do love accounts," Mrs. Bell admitted. "And I can keep run of things. I've often thought your Father'd have done better if he'd let me run that end of his business."

Diantha gave a fierce little laugh. She admired her father in some ways, enjoyed him in some ways, loved him as a child does if not ill-treated; but she loved her mother with a sort of passionate pity mixed with pride; feeling always nobler power in her than had ever had a fair chance to grow. It seemed to her an interminable dull tragedy; this graceful, eager, black-eyed woman, spending what to the girl was literally a lifetime, in the conscientious performance of duties she did not love.

She knew her mother's idea of duty, knew the clear head, the steady will, the active intelligence holding her relentlessly to the task; the chafe and fret of seeing her husband constantly attempting against her judgment, and failing for lack of the help he scorned. Young as she was, she realized that the nervous breakdown of these later years was wholly due to that common misery of "the square man in the round hole."

She folded her finished sheet in accurate lines and laid it away—taking her mother's also. "Now you sit still for once, Mother dear, read or lie down. Don't you stir till supper's ready."

And from pantry to table she stepped, swiftly and lightly, setting out what was needed, greased her pans and set them before her, and proceeded to make biscuit.

Her mother watched her admiringly. "How easy you do it!" she said. "I never could make bread without getting flour all over me. You don't spill a speck!"

Diantha smiled. "I ought to do it easily by this time. Father's got to have hot bread for supper—or thinks he has!—and I've made 'em—every night when I was at home for this ten years back!"

"I guess you have," said Mrs. Bell proudly. "You were only eleven when you made your first batch. I can remember just as well! I had one of my bad headaches that night—and it did seem as if I couldn't sit up! But your Father's got to have his biscuit whether or no. And you said, 'Now Mother you lie right still on that sofa and let me do it! I can!' And you could!—you did! They were bettern' mine that first time—and your Father praised 'em—and you've been at it ever since."

"Yes," said Diantha, with a deeper note of feeling than her mother caught, "I've been at it ever since!"

"Except when you were teaching school," pursued her mother.

"Except when I taught school at Medville," Diantha corrected. "When I taught here I made 'em just the same."

"So you did," agreed her mother. "So you did! No matter how tired you were—you wouldn't admit it. You always were the best child!"

"If I was tired it was not of making biscuits anyhow. I was tired enough of teaching school though. I've got something to tell you, presently, Mother."

She covered the biscuits with a light cloth and set them on the shelf over the stove; then poked among the greasewood roots to find what she wanted and started a fire. "Why *don't* you get an oil stove? Or a gasoline? It would be a lot easier."

"Yes," her mother agreed. "I've wanted one for twenty years; but you know your Father won't have one in the house. He says they're dangerous. What are you going to tell me, dear? I do hope you and Ross haven't quarrelled."

"No indeed we haven't, Mother. Ross is splendid. Only—"

"Only what, Dinah?"

"Only he's so tied up!" said the girl, brushing every chip from the hearth. "He's perfectly helpless there, with that mother of his—and those four sisters."

"Ross is a good son," said Mrs. Bell, "and a good brother. I never saw a better. He's certainly doing his duty. Now if his father'd lived you two could have got married by this time maybe, though you're too young yet."

Diantha washed and put away the dishes she had used, saw that the pantry was in its usual delicate order, and proceeded to set the table, with light steps and no clatter of dishes.

"I'm twenty-one," she said.

"Yes, you're twenty-one," her mother allowed. "It don't seem possible, but you are. My first baby!" she looked at her proudly.

"If Ross has to wait for all those girls to marry—and to pay his father's debts—I'll be old enough," said Diantha grimly.

Her mother watched her quick assured movements with admiration, and listened with keen sympathy. "I know it's hard, dear child. You've only been engaged six months—and it looks as if it might be some years before Ross'll be able to marry. He's got an awful load for a boy to carry alone."

"I should say he had!" Diantha burst forth. "Five helpless women!—or three women, and two girls. Though Cora's as old as I was when I began to teach. And not one of 'em will lift a finger to earn her own living."

"They weren't brought up that way," said Mrs. Bell. "Their mother don't approve of it. She thinks the home is the place for a woman—and so does Ross—and so do I," she added rather faintly.

Diantha put her pan of white puff-balls into the oven, sliced a quantity of smoked beef in thin shavings, and made white sauce for it, talking the while as if these acts were automatic. "I don't agree with Mrs. Warden on that point, nor with Ross, nor with you, Mother," she said, "What I've got to tell you is this—I'm going away from home. To work."

Mrs. Bell stopped rocking, stopped fanning, and regarded her daughter with wide frightened eyes.

"Why Diantha!" she said. "Why Diantha! You wouldn't go and leave your Mother!"

Diantha drew a deep breath and stood for a moment looking at the feeble little woman in the chair. Then she went to her, knelt down and hugged her close—close.

"It's not because I don't love you, Mother. It's because I do. And it's not because I don't love Ross either:—it's because I *do*. I want to take care of you, Mother, and make life easier for you as long as you live. I want to help him—to help carry that awful load—and I'm going—to—do—it!"

She stood up hastily, for a step sounded on the back porch. It was only her sister, who hurried in, put a dish on the table, kissed her mother and took another rocking-chair.

"I just ran in," said she, "to bring those berries. Aren't they beauties? The baby's asleep. Gerald hasn't got in yet. Supper's all ready, and I can see him coming time enough to run back. Why, Mother! What's the matter? You're crying!"

"Am I?" asked Mrs. Bell weakly; wiping her eyes in a dazed way.

"What are you doing to Mother, Diantha?" demanded young Mrs. Peters. "Bless me! I thought you and she never had any differences! I was always the black sheep, when I was at home. Maybe that's why I left so early!"

She looked very pretty and complacent, this young matron and mother of nineteen; and patted the older woman's hand affectionately, demanding, "Come—what's the trouble?"

"You might as well know now as later," said her sister. "I have decided to leave home, that's all."

"To leave home!" Mrs. Peters sat up straight and stared at her. "To leave home!—And Mother!"

"Well?" said Diantha, while the tears rose and ran over from her mother's eyes. "Well, why not? You left home—and Mother—before you were eighteen."

"That's different!" said her sister sharply. "I left to be married,—to have a home of my own. And besides I haven't gone far! I can see Mother every day."

"That's one reason I can go now better than later on," Diantha said. "You are close by in case of any trouble."

"What on earth are you going for? Ross isn't ready to marry yet, is he?"

"No—nor likely to be for years. That's another reason I'm going."

"But what *for,* for goodness sake."

"To earn money—for one thing."

"Can't you earn money enough by teaching?" the Mother broke in eagerly. "I know you haven't got the same place this fall—but you can get another easy enough."

Diantha shook her head. "No, Mother, I've had enough of

that. I've taught for four years. I don't like it, I don't do well, and it exhausts me horribly. And I should never get beyond a thousand or fifteen hundred dollars a year if I taught for a lifetime."

"Well, I declare!" said her sister. "What do you *expect* to get? I should think fifteen hundred dollars a year was enough for any woman!"

Diantha peered into the oven and turned her biscuit pan around.

"And you're meaning to leave home just to make money, are you?"

"Why not?" said Diantha firmly. "Henderson did—when he was eighteen. None of you blamed him."

"I don't see what that's got to do with it," her mother ventured. "Henderson's a boy, and boys have to go, of course. A mother expects that. But a girl—Why, Diantha! How can I get along without you! With my health!"

"I should think you'd be ashamed of yourself to think of such a thing!" said young Mrs. Peters.

A slow step sounded outside, and an elderly man, tall, slouching, carelessly dressed, entered, stumbling a little over the rag-mat at the door.

"Father hasn't got used to that rug in fourteen years!" said his youngest daughter laughingly. "And Mother will straighten it out after him! I'm bringing Gerald up on better principles. You should just see him wait on me!"

"A man should be master in his own household," Mr. Bell proclaimed, raising a dripping face from the basin and looking around for the towel—which his wife handed him.

"You won't have much household to be master of presently," said Mrs. Peters provokingly. "Half of it's going to leave."

Mr. Bell came out of his towel and looked from one to the other for some explanation of this attempted joke, "What nonsense are you talking?" he demanded.

"I think it's nonsense myself," said the pretty young woman—her hand on the doorknob. "But you'd better enjoy those biscuits of Di's while you can—you won't get many more!

There's Gerald—good night!" And off she ran.

Diantha set the plateful on the table, puffy, brown, and crisply crusted. "Supper's ready," she said. "Do sit down, Mother," and she held the chair for her. "Minnie's quite right, Father, though I meant not to tell you till you'd had supper. I am going away to work."

Mr. Bell regarded his daughter with a stern, slow stare; not so much surprised as annoyed by an untimely jesting. He ate a hot biscuit in two un-Fletcherized mouthfuls, and put more sugar in his large cup of tea. "You've got your Mother all worked up with your nonsense," said he. "What are you talking about anyway?"

Diantha met his eyes unflinchingly. He was a tall old man, still handsome and impressive in appearance, had been the head of his own household beyond question, ever since he was left the only son of an idolizing mother. But he had never succeeded in being the head of anything else. Repeated failures in the old New England home had resulted in his ruthlessly selling all the property there; and bringing his delicate wife and three young children to California. Vain were her protests and objections. It would do her good—best place in the world for children— good for nervous complaints too. A wife's duty was to follow her husband, of course. She had followed, willy nilly; and it was good for the children—there was no doubt of that.

Mr. Bell had profited little by his venture. They had the ranch, the flowers and fruit and ample living of that rich soil; but he had failed in oranges, failed in raisins, failed in prunes, and was now failing in wealth-promising hens.

But Mrs. Bell, though an ineffectual housekeeper, did not fail in the children. They had grown up big and vigorous, sturdy, handsome creatures, especially the two younger ones. Diantha was good-looking enough. Roscoe Warden thought her divinely beautiful. But her young strength had been heavily taxed from childhood in that complex process known as "helping mother." As a little child she had been of constant service in caring for the babies; and early developed such competence in the various arts of house work as filled her mother with fond pride, and even wrung from her father some grudging recognition. That he did not value it more was because he expected such competence in women, all women; it was their natural field of ability, their duty as wives and mothers. Also as daughters. If they failed in it that was by illness or perversity. If they succeeded—that was a matter of course.

He ate another of Diantha's excellent biscuits, his greyish-red whiskers slowly wagging; and continued to eye her disapprovingly. She said nothing, but tried to eat; and tried still harder to make her heart go quietly, her cheeks keep cool, and her eyes dry. Mrs. Bell also strove to keep a cheerful countenance; urged food upon her family; even tried to open some topic of conversation; but her gentle words trailed off into unnoticed silence.

Mr. Bell ate until he was satisfied and betook himself to a comfortable chair by the lamp, where he unfolded the smart local paper and lit his pipe. "When you've got through with the dishes, Diantha," he said coldly, "I'll hear about this proposition of yours."

Diantha cleared the table, lowered the leaves, set it back against the wall, spreading the turkey-red cloth upon it. She washed the dishes,—her kettle long since boiling, scalded them, wiped them, set them in their places; washed out the towels, wiped the pan and hung it up, swiftly, accurately, and with a quietness that would have seemed incredible to any mistress of heavy-footed servants. Then with heightened color and firm-set mouth, she took her place by the lamplit table and sat still.

Her mother was patiently darning large socks with many holes—a kind of work she specially disliked. "You'll have to get some new socks, Father," she ventured, "these are pretty well gone."

"O they'll do a good while yet," he replied, not looking at them. "I like your embroidery, my dear."

That pleased her. She did not like to embroider, but she did like to be praised.

Diantha took some socks and set to work, red-checked and

excited, but silent yet. Her mother's needle trembled irregularly under and over, and a tear or two slid down her cheeks.

Finally Mr. Bell laid down his finished paper and his emptied pipe and said, "Now then. Out with it."

This was not a felicitious opening. It is really astonishing how little diplomacy parents exhibit, how difficult they make it for the young to introduce a proposition. There was nothing for it but a bald statement, so Diantha made it baldly.

"I have decided to leave home and go to work," she said.

"Don't you have work enough to do at home?" he inquired, with the same air of quizzical superiority which had always annoyed her so intensely, even as a little child.

She would cut short this form of discussion: "I am going away to earn my living. I have given up school-teaching—I don't like it, and, there isn't money enough in it. I have plans—which will speak for themselves later."

"So," said Mr. Bell, "Plans all made, eh? I suppose you've considered your Mother in these plans?"

"I have," said his daughter. "It is largely on her account that I'm going."

"You think it'll be good for your Mother's health to lose your assistance, do you?"

"I know she'll miss me; but I haven't left the work on her shoulders. I am going to pay for a girl—to do the work I've done. It won't cost you any more, Father; and you'll save some— for she'll do the washing too. You didn't object to Henderson's going—at eighteen. You didn't object to Minnie's going—at seventeen. Why should you object to my going—at twenty-one."

"I haven't objected—so far," replied her father. "Have your plans also allowed for the affection and duty you owe your parents?"

"I have done my duty—as well as I know how," she answered. "Now I am twenty-one, and self-supporting—and have a right to go."

"O yes. You have a right—a legal right—if that's what you base your idea of a child's duty on! And while you're talking of

rights—how about a parent's rights? How about common gratitude! How about what you owe to me—for all the care and pains
and cost it's been to bring you up. A child's a rather expensive
investment these days."

Diantha flushed, she had expected this, and yet it struck her
like a blow. It was not the first time she had heard it—this claim
of filial obligation.

"I have considered that position, Father. I know you feel that
way—you've often made me feel it. So I've been at some pains
to work it out—on a money basis. Here is an account—as full
as I could make it." She handed him a paper covered with neat
figures. The totals read as follows:

> Miss Diantha Bell,
> To Mr. Henderson R. Bell, Dr.

> To medical and dental expenses. $110.00
> To school expenses. $76.00
> To clothing, in full $1,130.00
> To board and lodging at $3.00 a week $2,184.00
> To incidentals. $100.00
>
> _____
>
> $3.600.00

He studied the various items carefully, stroking his beard,
half in anger, half in unavoidable amusement. Perhaps there
was a tender feeling too, as he remembered that doctor's bill—
the first he ever paid, with the other, when she had scarlet fever;
and saw the exact price of the high chair which had served all
three of the children, but of which she magnanimously shoul-
dered the whole expense.

The clothing total was so large that it made him whistle—he
knew he had never spent $1,130.00 on one girl's clothes. But the
items explained it.

```
Materials, 3 years at an average of $10 a year . . . . . . .$30.00
Five years averaging $20 each year . . . . . . . . . . . . . .$100.00
Five years averaging $30 each year . . . . . . . . . . . . . .$50.00
Five years averaging $50 each year . . . . . . . . . . . . . .$250.00
                                                            ————
                                                            $530.00
```

The rest was "Mother's labor", averaging twenty full days a year at $2 a day, $40 a year. For fifteen years, $600.00. Mother's labor—on one child's, clothes—footing up to $600.00. It looked strange to see cash value attached to that unfailing source of family comfort and advantage.

The school expenses puzzled him a bit, for she had only gone to public schools; but she was counting books and slates and even pencils—it brought up evenings long passed by, the sewing wife, the studying children, the "Say, Father, I've got to have a new slate—mine's broke!"

"Broken, Dina," her Mother would gently correct, while he demanded, "How did you break it?" and scolded her for her careless tomboy ways. Slates—three, $1.50—they were all down. And slates didn't cost so much come to think of it, even the red-edged ones, wound with black, that she always wanted.

Board and lodging was put low, at $3.00 per week, but the items had a footnote as to house-rent in the country, and food raised on the farm. Yes, he guessed that was a full rate for the plain food and bare little bedroom they always had.

"It's what Aunt Esther paid the winter she was here," said Diantha.

```
Circuses—three . . . . . . . . . . . . . . . . . . . . . . . . . . . . .$1.50
Share in melodeon . . . . . . . . . . . . . . . . . . . . . . . . . .$50.00
```

Yes, she was one of five to use and enjoy it.

Music lessons. $30.00

And quite a large margin left here, called miscellaneous, which he smiled to observe made just an even figure, and suspected she had put in for that purpose as well as from generosity.

"This board account looks kind of funny," he said—"only fourteen years of it!"

"I didn't take table-board—nor a room—the first year—nor much the second. I've allowed $1.00 a week for that, and $2.00 for the third—that takes out two, you see. Then it's $156 a year till I was fourteen and earned board and wages, two more years at $156—and I've paid since I was seventeen, you know."

"Well—I guess you did—I guess you did." He grinned genially. "Yes," he continued slowly, "I guess that's a fair enough account. 'Cording to this, you owe me $3,600.00, young woman! I didn't think it cost that much to raise a girl."

"I know it," said she. "But here's the other side."

It was the other side. He had never once thought of such a side to the case. This account was as clear and honest as the first and full of exasperating detail. She laid before him the second sheet of figures and watched while he read, explaining hurriedly:

"It was a clear expense for ten years—not counting help with the babies. Then I began to do housework regularly—when I was ten or eleven, two hours a day; three when I was twelve and thirteen—real work you'd have had to pay for, and I've only put it at ten cents an hour. When Mother was sick the year I was fourteen, and I did it all but the washing—all a servant would have done for $3.00 a week. Ever since then I have done three hours a day outside of school, full grown work now, at twenty cents an hour. That's what we have to pay here, you know."

Thus it mounted up:

Mr. Henderson R. Bell,
To Miss Diantha Bell, Dr.

For labor and services!!!!!

Two years, two hours a day at 10c. an hour $146.00
Two years, three hours a day at 10c. an hour $219.00
One year, full wages at $5.00 a week $260.00
Six years and a half, three hours a day at 20c $1423.50

$2048.50

Mr. Bell meditated carefully on these figures. To think of that child's labor footing up to two thousand dollars and over! It was lucky a man had a wife and daughters to do this work, or he could never support a family.

Then came her school-teaching years. She had always been a fine scholar and he had felt very proud of his girl when she got a good school position in her eighteenth year.

California salaries were higher than eastern ones, and times had changed too; the year he taught school he remembered the salary was only $300.00—and he was a man. This girl got $600, next year $700, $800, $900; why it made $3,000 she had earned in four years. Astonishing. Out of this she had a balance in the bank of $550.00. He was pleased to see that she had been so saving. And her clothing account—little enough he admitted for four years and six months, $300.00. All incidentals for the whole time, $50.00—this with her balance made just $900. That left $2,100.00.

"Twenty-one hundred dollars unaccounted for, young lady!—besides this nest egg in the bank—I'd no idea you were so wealthy. What have you done with all that?"

"Given it to you, Father," said she quietly, and handed him the third sheet of figures.

Board and lodging at $4.00 a week for 4 1/2 years made

$936.00, that he could realize; but "cash advance" $1,164 more—he could not believe it. That time her mother was so sick and Diantha had paid both the doctor and the nurse—yes—he had been much cramped that year—and nurses come high. For Henderson, Jr.'s, expenses to San Francisco, and again for Henderson when he was out of a job—Mr. Bell remembered the boy's writing for the money, and his not having it, and Mrs. Bell saying she could arrange with Diantha.

Arrange! And that girl had kept this niggardly account of it! For Minnie's trip to the Yosemite—and what was this?—for his raisin experiment—for the new horse they simply had to have for the drying apparatus that year he lost so much money in apricots—and for the spraying materials—yes, he could not deny the items, and they covered that $1,164.00 exactly.

Then came the deadly balance, of the account between them:

Her labor	$2,047.00
Her board	$936.00
Her "cash advanced"	$1,164.00
	————
	$4,147.00
His expense for her	$3,600.00
	————
Due her from him.	$547.00

Diantha revolved her pencil between firm palms, and looked at him rather quizzically; while her mother rocked and darned and wiped away an occasional tear. She almost wished she had not kept accounts so well.

Mr. Bell pushed the papers away and started to his feet.

"This is the most shameful piece of calculation I ever saw in my life," said he. "I never heard of such a thing! You go and count up in cold dollars the work that every decent girl does for her family and is glad to! I wonder you haven't charged your mother for nursing her?"

"You notice I haven't," said Diantha coldly.

"And to think," said he, gripping the back of a chair and looking down at her fiercely, "to think that a girl who can earn nine hundred dollars a year teaching school, and stay at home and do her duty by her family besides, should plan to desert her mother outright—now she's old and sick! Of course I can't stop you! You're of age, and children nowadays have no sense of natural obligation after they're grown up. You can go, of course, and disgrace the family as you propose—but you needn't expect to have me consent to it or approve of it—or of you. It's a shameful thing—and you are an unnatural daughter—that's all I've got to say!"

Mr. Bell took his hat and went out—a conclusive form of punctuation much used by men in discussions of this sort.

CHAPTER III: BREAKERS

Duck! Dive! Here comes another one!
Wait till the crest-ruffles show!
Beyond is smooth water in beauty and wonder—
Shut your mouth! Hold your breath! Dip your head under!
Dive through the weight and the wash, and the thunder—
Look out for the undertow!

If Diantha imagined that her arithmetical victory over a too-sordid presentation of the parental claim was a final one, she soon found herself mistaken.

It is easy to say—putting an epic in an epigram—"She seen her duty and she done it!" but the space and time covered are generally as far beyond our plans as the estimates of an amateur mountain climber exceed his achievements.

Her determination was not concealed by her outraged family. Possibly they thought that if the matter was well aired, and generally discussed, the daring offender might reconsider. Well-aired it certainly was, and widely discussed by the parents of the little town before young people who sat in dumbness, or made faint defense. It was also discussed by the young people, but not before their parents.

She had told Ross, first of all, meaning to have a quiet talk with him to clear the ground before arousing her own family; but he was suddenly away just as she opened the subject, by a man on a wheel—some wretched business about the store of course—and sent word that night that he could not come up again. Couldn't come up the next night either. Two long days— two long evenings without seeing him. Well—if she went away she'd have to get used to that.

But she had so many things to explain, so much to say to make it right with him; she knew well what a blow it was. Now it was all over town—and she had had no chance to defend her position.

The neighbors called. Tall bony Mrs. Delafield who lived nearest to them and had known Diantha for some years, felt it her duty to make a special appeal—or attack rather; and brought with her stout Mrs. Schlosster, whose ancestors and traditions were evidently of German extraction.

Diantha retired to her room when she saw these two bearing down upon the house; but her mother called her to make a pitcher of lemonade for them—and having entered there was no escape. They harried her with questions, were increasingly offended by her reticence, and expressed disapproval with a fullness that overmastered the girl's self-control.

"I have as much right to go into business as any other citizen, Mrs. Delafield," she said with repressed intensity. "I am of age and live in a free country. What you say of children no longer applies to me."

"And what is this mysterious business you're goin' into—if one may inquire? Nothin you're ashamed to mention, I hope?" asked Mrs. Delafield.

"If a woman refuses to mention her age is it because she's ashamed of it?" the girl retorted, and Mrs. Delafield flushed darkly.

"Never have I heard such talk from a maiden to her elders," said Mrs. Schlosster. "In my country the young have more respect, as is right."

Mrs. Bell objected inwardly to any reprimand of her child by others; but she agreed to the principle advanced and made no comment.

Diantha listened to quite a volume of detailed criticism, inquiry and condemnation, and finally rose to her feet with the stiff courtesy of the young.

"You must excuse me now," she said with set lips. "I have some necessary work to do."

She marched upstairs, shut her bedroom door and locked it, raging inwardly. "Its none of their business! Not a shadow! Why should Mother sit there and let them talk to me like that! One would think childhood had no limit—unless it's matrimony!"

This reminded her of her younger sister's airs of superior wisdom, and did not conduce to a pleasanter frame of mind. "With all their miserable little conventions and idiocies! And what 'they'll say,' and 'they'll think'! As if I cared! Minnie'll be just such another!"

She heard the ladies going out, still talking continuously, a faint response from her mother now and then, a growing quiet as their steps receded toward the gate; and then another deeper voice took up the theme and heavily approached.

It was the minister! Diantha dropped into her rocker and held the arms tight. "Now I'll have to take it again I suppose. But he ought to know me well enough to understand."

"Diantha!" called her mother, "Here's Dr. Major;" and the girl washed her face and came down again.

Dr. Major was a heavy elderly man with a strong mouth and a warm hand clasp. "What's all this I hear about you, young lady?" he demanded, holding her hand and looking her straight in the eye. "Is this a new kind of Prodigal Daughter we're encountering?"

He did not look nor sound condemnatory, and as she faced him she caught a twinkle in the wise old eyes.

"You can call it that if you want to," she said, "Only I thought the Prodigal Son just spent his money—I'm going to earn some."

"I want you to talk to Diantha, Doctor Major," Mrs. Bell struck in. "I'm going to ask you to excuse me, and go and lie down for a little. I do believe she'll listen to you more than to anybody."

The mother retired, feeling sure that the good man who had known her daughter for over fifteen years would have a restraining influence now; and Diantha braced herself for the attack.

It came, heavy and solid, based on reason, religion, tradition, the custom of ages, the pastoral habit of control and protection, the father's instinct, the man's objection to a girl's adventure. But it was courteous, kind, and rationally put, and she met it point by point with the whole-souled arguments of a new position, the passionate enthusiasm of her years.

They called a truce.

"I can see that you *think* its your duty, young, woman—that's the main thing. I think you're wrong. But what you believe to be right you have to do. That's the way we learn my dear, that's the way we learn! Well—you've been a good child ever since I've known you. A remarkably good child. If you have to sow this kind of wild oats—" they both smiled at this, "I guess we can't stop you. I'll keep your secret—"

"Its not a secret really," the girl explained, "I'll tell them as soon as I'm settled. Then they can tell—if they want to." And they both smiled again.

"Well—I won't tell till I hear of it then. And—yes, I guess I can furnish that document with a clean conscience."

She gave him paper and pen and he wrote, with a grin, handing her the result.

She read it, a girlish giggle lightening the atmosphere. "Thank you!" she said earnestly. "Thank you ever so much. I knew you would help me."

"If you get stuck anywhere just let me know," he said rising. "This Proddy Gal may want a return ticket yet!"

"I'll walk first!" said Diantha.

"O Dr. Major," cried her mother from the window, "Don't go! We want you to stay to supper of course!"

But he had other calls to make, he said, and went away, his big hands clasped behind him; his head bent, smiling one minute and shaking his head the next.

Diantha leaned against a pearly eucalyptus trunk and watched him. She would miss Dr. Major. But who was this approaching? Her heart sank miserably. Mrs. Warden—and *all* the girls.

She went to meet them—perforce. Mrs. Warden had always been kind and courteous to her; the girls she had not seen very much of, but they had the sweet Southern manner, were always polite. Ross's mother she must love. Ross's sisters too—if she could. Why did the bottom drop out of her courage at sight of them?

"You dear child!" said Mrs. Warden, kissing her. "I know just how you feel! You want to help my boy! That's your secret! But this won't do it, my dear!"

"You've no idea how badly Ross feels!" said Madeline. "Mrs. Delafield dropped in just now and told us. You ought to have seen him!"

"He didn't believe it of course," Adeline put in. "And he wouldn't say a thing—not a thing to blame you."

"We said we'd come over right off—and tried to bring him—but he said he'd got to go back to the store," Coraline explained.

"He was mad though!" said Dora—"*I* know."

Diantha looked from one to the other helplessly.

"Come in! Come in!" said Mrs. Bell hospitably. "Have this rocker, Mrs. Warden—wouldn't you like some cool drink? Diantha?"

"No indeed!" Mrs. Warden protested. "Don't get a thing. We're going right back, it's near supper time. No, we can't think of staying, of course not, no indeed!—But we had to come over and hear about this dear child's idea!—Now tell us all about it, Diantha!"

There they sat—five pairs of curious eyes—and her mother's

sad ones—all kind—all utterly incapable of understanding.

She moistened her lips and plunged desperately. "It is nothing dreadful, Mrs. Warden. Plenty of girls go away to earn their livings nowadays. That is all I'm doing."

"But why go away?"

"I thought you were earning your living before!"

"Isn't teaching earning your living?"

"What *are* you going to do?" the girls protested variously, and Mrs. Warden, with a motherly smile, suggested!!!!!

"That doesn't explain your wanting to leave Ross, my dear—and your mother!"

"I don't want to leave them," protested Diantha, trying to keep her voice steady. "It is simply that I have made up my mind I can do better elsewhere."

"Do what better?" asked Mrs. Warden with sweet patience, which reduced Diantha to the bald statement, "Earn more money in less time."

"And is that better than staying with your mother and your lover?" pursued the gentle inquisitor; while the girls tried, "What do you want to earn more money for?" and "I thought you earned a lot before."

Now Diantha did not wish to state in so many words that she wanted more money in order to marry sooner—she had hardly put it to herself that way. She could not make them see in a few moments that her plan was to do far more for her mother than she would otherwise ever be able to. And as to making them understand the larger principles at stake—the range and depth of her full purpose—that would be physically impossible.

"I am sorry!" she said with trembling lips. "I am extremely sorry. But—I cannot explain!"

Mrs. Warden drew herself up a little. "Cannot explain to me?—Your mother, of course, knows?"

"Diantha is naturally more frank with me than with—anyone," said Mrs. Bell proudly, "But she does not wish her—business—plans—made public at present!"

Her daughter looked at her with vivid gratitude, but the words "made public" were a little unfortunate perhaps.

"Of course," Mrs. Warden agreed, with her charming smile, "that we can quite understand. I'm sure I should always wish my girls to feel so. Madeline—just show Mrs. Bell that necktie you're making—she was asking about the stitch, you remember."

The necktie was produced and admired, while the other girls asked Diantha if she had her fall dressmaking done yet—and whether she found wash ribbon satisfactory. And presently the whole graceful family withdrew, only Dora holding her head with visible stiffness.

Diantha sat on the floor by her mother, put her head in her lap and cried. "How splendid of you, Mother!" she sobbed. "How simply splendid! I will tell you now—if—if—you won't tell even Father—yet."

"Dear child" said her Mother, "I'd rather not know in that case. It is—easier."

"That's what I kept still for!" said the girl. "It's hard enough, goodness knows—as it is! Its nothing wicked, or even risky, Mother dear—and as far as I can see it is right!"

Her mother smiled through her tears. "If you say that, my dear child, I know there's no stopping you. And I hate to argue with you—even for your own sake, because it is so much to my advantage to have you here. I—shall miss you—Diantha!"

"Don't, Mother!" sobbed the girl.

"Its natural for the young to go. We expect it—in time. But you are so young yet—and—well, I had hoped the teaching would satisfy you till Ross was ready."

Diantha sat up straight.

"Mother! can't you see Ross'll never be ready! Look at that family! And the way they live! And those mortgages! I could wait and teach and save a little even with Father always losing money; but I can't see Ross wearing himself out for years and years—I just *can't* bear it!"

Her mother stroked her fair hair softly, not surprised that her own plea was so lost in thought of the brave young lover.

"And besides," the girl went on "If I waited—and saved—

and married Ross—what becomes of *you,* I'd like to know? What I can't stand is to have you grow older and sicker—and never have any good time in all your life!"

Mrs. Bell smiled tenderly. "You dear child!" she said; as if an affectionate five-year old had offered to get her a rainbow, "I know you mean it all for the best. But, O my *dearest*! I'd rather have you—here—at home with me—than any other 'good time' you can imagine!"

She could not see the suffering in her daughter's face; but she felt she had made an impression, and followed it up with heartbreaking sincerity. She caught the girl to her breast and held her like a little child. "O my baby! my baby! Don't leave your mother. I can't bear it!"

A familiar step outside, heavy, yet uncertain, and they both looked at each other with frightened eyes.

They had forgotten the biscuit.

"Supper ready?" asked Mr. Bell, with grim humor.

"It will be in a moment, Father," cried Diantha springing to her feet. "At least—in a few moments."

"Don't fret the child, Father," said Mrs. Henderson softly. "She's feeling bad enough."

"Sh'd think she would," replied her husband. "Moreover—to my mind—she ought to."

He got out the small damp local paper and his pipe, and composed himself in obvious patience: yet somehow this patience seemed to fill the kitchen, and to act like a ball and chain to Diantha's feet.

She got supper ready, at last, making griddle-cakes instead of biscuit, and no comment was made of the change: but the tension in the atmosphere was sharply felt by the two women; and possibly by the tall old man, who ate less than usual, and said absolutely nothing.

"I'm going over to see Edwards about that new incubator," he said when the meal was over, and departed; and Mrs. Bell, after trying in vain to do her mending, wiped her clouded glasses and went to bed.

Diantha made all neat and tidy; washed her own wet eyes again, and went out under the moon. In that broad tender mellow light she drew a deep breath and stretched her strong young arms toward the sky in dumb appeal.

"I knew it would be hard," she murmured to herself, "That is I knew the facts—but I didn't know the feeling!"

She stood at the gate between the cypresses, sat waiting under the acacia boughs, walked restlessly up and down the path outside, the dry pepper berries crush softly under foot; bracing herself for one more struggle—and the hardest of all.

"He will understand!" he told herself, over and over, but at the bottom of her heart she knew he wouldn't.

He came at last; a slower, wearier step than usual; came and took both her hands in his and stood holding them, looking at her questioningly. Then he held her face between his palms and made her look at him. Her eyes were brave and steady, but the mouth trembled in spite of her.

He stilled it with a kiss, and drew her to a seat on the bench beside him. "My poor Little Girl! You haven't had a chance yet to really tell me about this thing, and I want you to right now. Then I'm going to kill about forty people in this town! *Somebody* has been mighty foolish."

She squeezed his hand, but found it very difficult to speak. His love, his sympathy, his tenderness, were so delicious after this day's trials—and before those further ones she could so well anticipate. She didn't wish to cry any more, that would by no means strengthen her position, and she found she couldn't seem to speak without crying.

"One would think to hear the good people of this town that you were about to leave home and mother for—well, for a trip to the moon!" he added. "There isn't any agreement as to what you're going to do, but they're unanimous as to its being entirely wrong. Now suppose you tell me about it."

"I will," said Diantha. "I began to the other night, you know, you first of course—it was too bad! your having to go off at that exact moment. Then I had to tell mother—because—well you'll see presently. Now dear—just let me say it *all*—before you—do anything."

"Say away, my darling. I trust you perfectly."

She flashed a grateful look at him. "It is this way, my dear. I have two, three, yes four, things to consider:—My own personal problem—my family's—yours—and a social one."

"My family's?" he asked, with a faint shade of offence in his tone.

"No no dear—your own," she explained.

"Better cut mine out, Little Girl," he said. "I'll consider that myself."

"Well—I won't talk about it if you don't want me to. There are the other three."

"I won't question your second, nor your imposing third, but isn't the first one—your own personal problem—a good deal answered?" he suggested, holding her close for a moment.

"Don't!" she said. "I can't talk straight when you put it that way."

She rose hurriedly and took a step or two up and down. "I don't suppose—in spite of your loving me, that I can make you see it as I do. But I'll be just as clear as I can. There are some years before us before we can be together. In that time I intend to go away and undertake a business I am interested in. My purpose is to—develop the work, to earn money, to help my family, and to—well, not to hinder you."

"I don't understand, I confess," he said. "Don't you propose to tell me what this 'work' is?"

"Yes—I will—certainly. But not yet dear! Let me try to show you how I feel about it."

"Wait," said he. "One thing I want to be sure of. Are you doing this with any quixotic notion of helping me—in *my* business? Helping me to take care of my family? Helping me to—" he stood up now, looking very tall and rather forbidding, "No, I won't say that to you."

"Would there be anything wrong in my meaning exactly that?" she asked, holding her own head a little higher; "both what you said and what you didn't?"

"It would be absolutely wrong, all of it," he answered. "I cannot believe that the woman I love would—could take such a position."

"Look here, Ross!" said the girl earnestly. "Suppose you knew where there was a gold mine—*knew it*—and by going away for a few years you could get a real fortune—wouldn't you do it?"

"Naturally I should," he agreed.

"Well, suppose it wasn't a gold mine, but a business, a new system like those cigar stores—or—some patent amusement specialty—or *anything*—that you knew was better than what you're doing—wouldn't you have a right to try it?"

"Of course I should—but what has that to do with this case?"

"Why it's the same thing! Don't you see? I have plans that will be of real benefit to all of us, something worth while to *do*—and not only for us but for *everybody*—a real piece of progress—and I'm going to leave my people—and even you!—for a little while—to make us all happier later on."

He smiled lovingly at her but shook his head slowly. "You dear, brave, foolish child!" he said. "I don't for one moment doubt your noble purposes. But you don't get the man's point of view—naturally. What's more you don't seem to get the woman's."

"Can you see no other point of view than those?" she asked.

"There are no others," he answered. "Come! come! my darling, don't add this new difficulty to what we've got to carry! I know you have a hard time of it at home. Some day, please God, you shall have an easier one! And I'm having a hard time too—I don't deny it. But you are the greatest joy and comfort I have, dear—you know that. If you go away—it will be harder and slower and longer—that's all. I shall have you to worry about too. Let somebody else do the gold-mine, dear—you stay here and comfort your Mother as long as you can—and me. How can I get along without you?"

He tried to put his arm around her again, but she drew back.

"Dear," she said. "If I deliberately do what I think is right—against your wishes—what will you do?"

"Do?" The laughed bitterly. "What can I do? I'm tied by the leg here—I can't go after you. I've nothing to pull you out of a scrape with if you get in one. I couldn't do anything but—stand it."

"And if I go ahead, and do what you don't like—and make you—suffer—would you—would you rather be free?" Her voice was very low and shaken, but he heard her well enough.

"Free of you? Free of *you*?" He caught her and held her and kissed her over and over.

"You are mine!" he said. "You have given yourself to me! You cannot leave me. Neither of us is free—ever again." But she struggled away from him.

"Both of us are free—to do what we think right, *always* Ross! I wouldn't try to stop you if you thought it was your duty to go to the North Pole!" She held him a little way off. "Let me tell you, dear. Sit down—let me tell you all about it." But he wouldn't sit down.

"I don't think I want to know the details," he said. "It doesn't much matter what you're going to do—if you really go away. I can't stop you—I see that. If you think this thing is your 'duty' you'll do it if it kills us all—and you too! If you have to go—I shall do nothing—can do nothing—but wait till you come back to me! Whatever happens, darling—no matter how you fail—don't ever be afraid to come back to me."

He folded his arms now—did not attempt to hold her—gave her the freedom she asked and promised her the love she had almost feared to lose—and her whole carefully constructed plan seemed like a child's sand castle for a moment; her heroic decision the wildest folly.

He was not even looking at her; she saw his strong, clean-cut profile dark against the moonlit house, a settled patience in its lines. Duty! Here was duty, surely, with tenderest happiness. She was leaning toward him—her hand was seeking his, when she heard through the fragrant silence a sound from her mother's room—the faint creak of her light rocking chair. She could not sleep—she was sitting up with her trouble, bearing it quietly as she had so many others.

The quiet everyday tragedy of that distasteful life—the slow withering away of youth and hope and ambition into a gray waste of ineffectual submissive labor—not only of her life, but of thousands upon thousands like her—it all rose up like a flood in the girl's hot young heart.

Ross had turned to her—was holding out his arms to her. "You won't go, my darling!" he said.

"I am going Wednesday on the 7.10," said Diantha.

CHAPTER IV: A CRYING NEED

"Lovest thou me?" said the Fair Ladye;
And the Lover he said, "Yea!"
"Then climb this tree—for my sake," said she,
"And climb it every day!"

So from dawn till dark he abrazed the bark
And wore his clothes away;
Till, "What has this tree to do with thee?"
The Lover at last did say.

It was a poor dinner. Cold in the first place, because Isabel would wait to thoroughly wash her long artistic hands; and put on another dress. She hated the smell of cooking in her garments; hated it worse on her white fingers; and now to look at the graceful erect figure, the round throat with the silver necklace about it, the soft smooth hair, silver-filletted, the negative beauty of the dove-colored gown, specially designed for home evenings, one would never dream she had set the table so well—and cooked the steak so abominably.

Isabel was never a cook. In the many servantless gaps of domestic life in Orchardina, there was always a strained atmosphere in the Porne household.

"Dear," said Mr. Porne, "might I petition to have the steak less cooked? I know you don't like to do it, so why not shorten the process?"

"I'm sorry," she answered, "I always forget about the steak from one time to the next."

"Yet we've had it three times this week, my dear."

"I thought you liked it better than anything," she with marked gentleness. "I'll get you other things—oftener."

"It's a shame you should have this to do, Isabel. I never meant you should cook for me. Indeed I didn't dream you cared so little about it."

"And I never dreamed you cared so much about it," she replied, still with repression. "I'm not complaining, am I? I'm only sorry you should be disappointed in me."

"It's not *you,* dear girl! You're all right! It's just this ever-lasting bother. Can't you get *anybody* that will stay?"

"I can't seem to get anybody on any terms, so far. I'm going again, to-morrow. Cheer up, dear—the baby keeps well—that's the main thing."

He sat on the rose-bowered porch and smoked while she cleared the table. At first he had tried to help her on these occasions, but their methods were dissimilar and she frankly told him she preferred to do it alone.

So she slipped off the silk and put on the gingham again, washed the dishes with the labored accuracy of a trained mind doing unfamiliar work, made the bread, redressed at last, and joined him about nine o'clock.

"It's too late to go anywhere, I suppose?" he ventured.

"Yes—and I'm too tired. Besides—we can't leave Eddie alone."

"O yes—I forget. Of course we can't."

His hand stole out to take hers. "I *am* sorry, dear. It's awfully rough on you women out here. How do they all stand it?"

"Most of them stand it much better than I do, Ned. You see they don't want to be doing anything else."

"Yes. That's the mischief of it!" he agreed; and she looked at him in the clear moonlight, wondering exactly what he thought the mischief was.

"Shall we go in and read a bit?" he offered; but she thought not.

"I'm too tired, I'm afraid. And Eddie'll wake up as soon as we begin."

So they sat awhile enjoying the soft silence, and the rich flower scents about them, till Eddie did wake presently, and Isabel went upstairs.

She slept little that night, lying quite still, listening to her husband's regular breathing so near her, and the lighter sound from the crib. "I am a very happy woman," she told herself resolutely; but there was no outpouring sense of love and joy. She knew she was happy, but by no means felt it. So she stared at the moon shadows and thought it over.

She had planned the little house herself, with such love, such hope, such tender happy care! Not her first work, which won high praise in the school in Paris, not the prize-winning plan for the library, now gracing Orchardina's prettiest square, was as dear to her as this most womanly task—the making of a home.

It was the library success which brought her here, fresh from her foreign studies, and Orchardina accepted with western cordiality the youth and beauty of the young architect, though a bit surprised at first that "I. H. Wright" was an Isabel. In her further work of overseeing the construction of that library, she had met Edgar Porne, one of the numerous eager young real estate men of that region, who showed a liberal enthusiasm for the general capacity of women in the professions, and a much warmer feeling for the personal attractions of this one.

Together they chose the lot on pepper-shaded Inez Avenue; together they watched the rising of the concrete walls and planned the garden walks and seats, and the tiny precious pool in the far corner. He was so sympathetic! so admiring! He took as much pride in the big "drawing room" on the third floor as she did herself. "Architecture is such fine work to do at home!"

they had both agreed. "Here you have your north light—your big table—plenty of room for work! You will grow famouser and famouser," he had lovingly insisted. And she had answered, "I fear I shall be too contented, dear, to want to be famous."

That was only some year and a-half ago,—but Isabel, lying there by her sleeping husband and sleeping child, was stark awake and only by assertion happy. She was thinking, persistently, of dust. She loved a delicate cleanliness. Her art was a precise one, her studio a workshop of white paper and fine pointed hard pencils, her painting the mechanical perfection of an even wash of color. And she saw, through the floors and walls and the darkness, the dust in the little shaded parlor—two days' dust at least, and Orchardina is very dusty!—dust in the dining-room gathered since yesterday—the dust in the kitchen—she would not count time there, and the dust—here she counted it inexorably—the dust of eight days in her great, light workroom upstairs. Eight days since she had found time to go up there.

Lying there, wide-eyed and motionless, she stood outside in thought and looked at the house—as she used to look at it with him, before they were married. Then, it had roused every blessed hope and dream of wedded joy—it seemed a casket of uncounted treasures. Now, in this dreary mood, it seemed not only a mere workshop, but one of alien tasks, continuous, impossible, like those set for the Imprisoned Princess by bad fairies in the old tales. In thought she entered the well-proportioned door—the Gate of Happiness—and a musty smell greeted her—she had forgotten to throw out those flowers! She turned to the parlor—no, the piano keys were gritty, one had to clean them twice a day to keep that room as she liked it.

From room to room she flitted, in her mind, trying to recall the exquisite things they meant to her when she had planned them; and each one now opened glaring and blank, as a place to work in—and the work undone.

"If I were an abler woman!" she breathed. And then her common sense and common honesty made her reply to herself: "I am able enough—in my own work! Nobody can do everything. I don't believe Edgar'd do it any better than I do.—He don't have to!"—and then such a wave of bitterness rushed over her that she was afraid, and reached out one hand to touch the crib—the other to her husband.

He awakened instantly. "What is it, Dear?" he asked. "Too tired to sleep, you poor darling? But you do love me a little, don't you?"

"O *yes!*" she answered. "I do. Of *course* I do! I'm just tired, I guess. Goodnight, Sweetheart."

She was late in getting to sleep and late in waking.

When he finally sat down to the hurriedly spread breakfast-table, Mr. Porne, long coffeeless, found it a bit difficult to keep his temper. Isabel was a little stiff, bringing in dishes and cups, and paying no attention to the sounds of wailing from above.

"Well if you won't I will!" burst forth the father at last, and ran upstairs, returning presently with a fine boy of some eleven months, who ceased to bawl in these familiar arms, and contented himself, for the moment, with a teaspoon.

"Aren't you going to feed him?" asked Mr. Porne, with forced patience.

"It isn't time yet," she announced wearily. "He has to have his bath first."

"Well," with a patience evidently forced farther, "isn't it time to feed me?"

"I'm very sorry," she said. "The oatmeal is burned again. You'll have to eat cornflakes. And—the cream is sour—the ice didn't come—or at least, perhaps I was out when it came—and then I forgot it..... I had to go to the employment agency in the morning!.... I'm sorry I'm so—so incompetent."

"So am I," he commented drily. "Are there any crackers for instance? And how about coffee?"

She brought the coffee, such as it was, and a can of condensed milk. Also crackers, and fruit. She took the baby and sat silent.

"Shall I come home to lunch?" he asked.

"Perhaps you'd better not," she replied coldly.

"Is there to be any dinner?"

"Dinner will be ready at six-thirty, if I have to get it myself."

"If you have to get it yourself I'll allow for seven-thirty," said he, trying to be cheerful, though she seemed little pleased by it. "Now don't take it so hard, Ellie. You are a first-class architect, anyhow—one can't be everything. We'll get another girl in time. This is just the common lot out here. All the women have the same trouble."

"Most women seem better able to meet it!" she burst forth. "It's not my trade! I'm willing to work, I like to work, but I can't *bear* housework! I can't seem to learn it at all! And the servants will not do it properly!"

"Perhaps they know your limitations, and take advantage of them! But cheer up, dear. It's no killing matter. Order by phone, don't forget the ice, and I'll try to get home early and help. Don't cry, dear girl, I love you, even if you aren't a good cook! And you love me, don't you?"

He kissed her till she had to smile back at him and give him a loving hug; but after he had gone, the gloom settled upon her spirits once more. She bathed the baby, fed him, put him to sleep; and came back to the table. The screen door had been left ajar and the house was buzzing with flies, hot, with a week's accumulating disorder. The bread she made last night in fear and trembling, was hanging fatly over the pans; perhaps sour already. She clapped it into the oven and turned on the heat.

Then she stood, undetermined, looking about that messy kitchen while the big flies bumped and buzzed on the windows, settled on every dish, and swung in giddy circles in the middle of the room. Turning swiftly she shut the door on them. The dining-room was nearly as bad. She began to put the cups and plates together for removal; but set her tray down suddenly and went into the comparative coolness of the parlor, closing the dining-room door behind her.

She was quite tired enough to cry after several nights of broken rest and days of constant discomfort and irritation; but a sense of rising anger kept the tears back.

"Of course I love him!" she said to herself aloud but softly, remembering the baby, "And no doubt he loves me! I'm glad to be his wife! I'm glad to be a mother to his child! I'm glad I married him! But—*this* is not what he offered! And it's not what I undertook! He hasn't had to change his business!"

She marched up and down the scant space, and then stopped short and laughed drily, continuing her smothered soliloquy.

"'Do you love me?' they ask, and, 'I will make you happy!' they say; and you get married—and after that it's Housework!"

"They don't say, 'Will you be my Cook?' 'Will you be my Chamber maid?' 'Will you give up a good clean well-paid business that you love—that has big hope and power and beauty in it—and come and keep house for me?'"

"Love him? I'd be in Paris this minute if I didn't! What has 'love' to do with dust and grease and flies!"

Then she did drop on the small sofa and cry tempestuously for a little while; but soon arose, fiercely ashamed of her weakness, and faced the day; thinking of the old lady who had so much to do she couldn't think what to first—so she sat down and made a pincushion.

Then—where to begin!

"Eddie will sleep till half-past ten—if I'm lucky. It's now nearly half-past nine," she meditated aloud. "If I do the upstairs work I might wake him. I mustn't forget the bread, the dishes, the parlor—O those flies! Well—I'll clear the table first!"

Stepping softly, and handling the dishes with slow care, she cleaned the breakfast table and darkened the dining-room, flapping out some of the flies with a towel. Then she essayed the parlor, dusting and arranging with undecided steps. "It *ought* to be swept," she admitted to herself; "I can't do it—there isn't time. I'll make it dark—"

"I'd rather plan a dozen houses!" she fiercely muttered, as she fussed about. "Yes—I'd rather build 'em—than to keep one clean!"

Then were her hopes dashed by a rising wail from above. She sat quite still awhile, hoping against hope that he would sleep again; but he wouldn't. So she brought him down in full cry.

In her low chair by the window she held him and produced bright and jingling objects from the tall workbasket that stood near by, sighing again as she glanced at its accumulated mending.

Master Eddy grew calm and happy in her arms, but showed a growing interest in the pleasing materials produced for his amusement, and a desire for closer acquaintance. Then a penetrating odor filled the air, and with a sudden "O dear!" she rose, put the baby on the sofa, and started toward the kitchen.

At this moment the doorbell rang.

Mrs. Porne stopped in her tracks and looked at the door. It remained opaque and immovable. She looked at the baby— who jiggled his spools and crowed. Then she flew to the oven and dragged forth the bread, not much burned after all. Then she opened the door.

A nice looking young woman stood before her, in a plain travelling suit, holding a cheap dress-suit case in one hand and a denim "roll-bag" in the other, who met her with a cheerful inquiring smile.

"Are you Mrs. Edgar Porne?" she asked.

"I am," answered that lady, somewhat shortly, her hand on the doorknob, her ear on the baby, her nose still remorsefully in the kitchen, her eyes fixed sternly on her visitor the while; as she wondered whether it was literature, cosmetics, or medicine.

She was about to add that she didn't want anything, when the young lady produced a card from the Rev. Benjamin A. Miner, Mrs. Porne's particularly revered minister, and stated that she had heard there was a vacancy in her kitchen and she would like the place.

"Introducing Mrs. D. Bell, well known to friends of mine."

"I don't know—" said Mrs. Porne, reading the card without in the least grasping what it said. "I—"

Just then there was a dull falling sound followed by a sharp rising one, and she rushed into the parlor without more words.

When she could hear and be heard again, she found Mrs. Bell

seated in the shadowy little hall, serene and cool. "I called on Mr. Miner yesterday when I arrived," said she, "with letters of introduction from my former minister, told him what I wanted to do, and asked him if he could suggest anyone in immediate need of help in this line. He said he had called here recently, and believed you were looking for someone. Here is the letter I showed him," and she handed Mrs. Porne a most friendly and appreciative recommendation of Miss D. Bell by a minister in Jopalez, Inca Co., stating that the bearer was fully qualified to do all kinds of housework, experienced, honest, kind, had worked seven years in one place, and only left it hoping to do better in Southern California.

Backed by her own pastor's approval this seemed to Mrs. Porne fully sufficient. The look of the girl pleased her, though suspiciously above her station in manner; service of any sort was scarce and high in Orchardina, and she had been an agelong week without any. "When can you come?" she asked.

"I can stop now if you like," said the stranger. "This is my baggage. But we must arrange terms first. If you like to try me I will come this week from noon to-day to noon next Friday, for seven dollars, and then if you are satisfied with my work we can make further arrangements. I do not do laundry work, of course, and don't undertake to have any care of the baby."

"I take care of my baby myself!" said Mrs. Porne, thinking the new girl was presuming, though her manner was most gently respectful. But a week was not long, she was well recommended, and the immediate pressure in that kitchen where the harvest was so ripe and the laborers so few—"Well—you may try the week," she said. "I'll show you your room. And what is your name?"

"Miss Bell."

CHAPTER V

When the fig growns on the thistle,
And the silk purse on the sow;
When one swallow brings the summer,
And blue moons on her brow!!!!!

Then we may look for strength and skill,
Experience, good health, good will,
Art and science well combined,
Honest soul and able mind,
Servants built upon this plan,
One to wait on every man,
Patiently from youth to age,—
For less than a street cleaner's wage!

When the parson's gay on Mondays,
When we meet a month of Sundays,
We may look for them and find them—
But Not Now!

When young Mrs. Weatherstone swept her trailing crepe from the automobile to her friend's door, it was opened by a quick, soft-footed maid with a pleasant face, who showed her into a parlor, not only cool and flower-lit, but having that fresh smell that tells of new-washed floors.

Mrs. Porne came flying down to meet her, with such a look of rest and comfort as roused instant notice.

"Why, Belle! I haven't seen you look so bright in ever so long. It must be the new maid!"

"That's it—she's 'Bell' too—'Miss Bell' if you please!"

The visitor looked puzzled. "Is she a—a friend?" she ventured, not sure of her ground.

"I should say she was! A friend in need! Sit here by the

window, Viva—and I'll tell you all about it—as far as it goes."

She gaily recounted her climax of confusion and weariness, and the sudden appearance of this ministering angel. "She arrived at about quarter of ten. I engaged her inside of five minutes. She was into a gingham gown and at work by ten o'clock!"

"What promptness! And I suppose there was plenty to do!"

Mrs. Porne laughed unblushingly. "There was enough for ten women it seemed to me! Let's see—it's about five now—seven hours. We have nine rooms, besides the halls and stairs, and my shop. She hasn't touched that yet. But the house is clean— *clean*! Smell it!"

She took her guest out into the hall, through the library and dining-room, upstairs where the pleasant bedrooms stretched open and orderly.

"She said that if I didn't mind she'd give it a superficial general cleaning today and be more thorough later!"

Mrs. Weatherstone looked about her with a rather languid interest. "I'm very glad for you, Belle, dear—but—what an endless nuisance it all is—don't you think so?"

"Nuisance! It's slow death! to me at least," Mrs. Porne answered. "But I don't see why you should mind. I thought Madam Weatherstone ran that—palace, of yours, and you didn't have any trouble at all."

"Oh yes, she runs it. I couldn't get along with her at all if she didn't. That's her life. It was my mother's too. Always fussing and fussing. Their houses on their backs—like snails!"

"Don't see why, with ten (or is it fifteen?) servants."

"Its twenty, I think. But my dear Belle, if you imagine that when you have twenty servants you have neither work nor care—come and try it awhile, that's all!"

"Not for a millionaire baby's ransom!" answered Isabel promptly.

"Give me my drawing tools and plans and I'm happy—but this business"—she swept a white hand wearily about—"it's not my work, that's all."

"But you *enjoy* it, don't you—I mean having nice things?" asked her friend.

"Of course I enjoy it, but so does Edgar. Can't a woman enjoy her home, just as a man does, without running the shop? I enjoy ocean travel, but I don't want to be either a captain or a common sailor!"

Mrs. Weatherstone smiled, a little sadly. "You're lucky, you have other interests," she said. "How about our bungalow? have you got any farther?"

Mrs. Porne flushed. "I'm sorry, Viva. You ought to have given it to someone else. I haven't gone into that workroom for eight solid days. No help, and the baby, you know. And I was always dog-tired."

"That's all right, dear, there's no very great rush. You can get at it now, can't you—with this other Belle to the fore?"

"She's not Belle, bless you—she's 'Miss Bell.' It's her last name."

Mrs. Weatherstone smiled her faint smile. "Well—why not? Like a seamstress, I suppose."

"Exactly." That's what she said. "If this labor was as important as that of seamstress or governess why not the same courtesy—Oh she's a most superior *and* opinionated young person, I can see that."

"I like her looks," admitted Mrs. Weatherstone, "but can't we look over those plans again; there's something I wanted to suggest." And they went up to the big room on the third floor.

In her shop and at her work Isabel Porne was a different woman. She was eager and yet calm; full of ideas and ideals, yet with a practical knowledge of details that made her houses dear to the souls of women.

She pointed out in the new drawings the practical advantages of kitchen and pantry; the simple but thorough ventilation, the deep closets, till her friend fairly laughed at her. "And you say you're not domestic!"

"I'm a domestic architect, if you like," said Isabel; "but not a domestic servant.—I'll remember what you say about those windows—it's a good idea," and she made a careful note of Mrs. Weatherstone's suggestion.

That lady pushed the plans away from her, and went to the many cushioned lounge in the wide west window, where she sat so long silent that Isabel followed at last and took her hand.

"Did you love him so much?" she asked softly.

"Who?" was the surprising answer.

"Why—Mr. Weatherstone," said Mrs. Porne.

"No—not very much. But he was something."

Isabel was puzzled. "I knew you so well in school," she said, "and that gay year in Paris. You were always a dear, submissive quiet little thing—but not like this. What's happened, Viva?"

"Nothing that anybody can help," said her friend. "Nothing that matters. What does matter, anyway? Fuss and fuss and fuss. Dress and entertain. Travel till you're tired, and rest till you're crazy! Then—when a real thing happens—there's all this!" and she lifted her black draperies disdainfully. "And mourning notepaper and cards and servant's livery—and all the things you mustn't do!"

Isabel put an arm around her. "Don't mind, dear—you'll get over this—you are young enough yet—the world is full of things to do!"

But Mrs. Weatherstone only smiled her faint smile again. "I loved another man, first," she said. "A real one. He died. He never cared for me at all. I cared for nothing else—nothing in life. That's why I married Martin Weatherstone—not for his old millions—but he really cared—and I was sorry for him. Now he's dead. And I'm wearing this—and still mourning for the other one."

Isabel held her hand, stroked it softly, laid it against her cheek.

"Oh, I'll feel differently in time, perhaps!" said her visitor.

"Maybe if you took hold of the house—if you ran things yourself,"—ventured Mrs. Porne.

Mrs. Weatherstone laughed. "And turn out the old lady? You don't know her. Why she managed her son till he ran away from her—and after he got so rich and imported her from Philadelphia to rule over Orchardina in general and his household in particular, she managed that poor little first wife of his into her grave, and that wretched boy—he's the only person that manages her! She's utterly spoiled him—that was his father's constant grief. No, no—let her run the house—she thinks she owns it."

"She's fond of you, isn't she?" asked Mrs. Porne.

"O I guess so—if I let her have her own way. And she certainly saves me a great deal of trouble. Speaking of trouble, there they are—she said she'd stop for me."

At the gate puffed the big car, a person in livery rang the bell, and Mrs. Weatherstone kissed her friend warmly, and passed like a heavy shadow along the rose-bordered path. In the tonneau sat a massive old lady in sober silks, with a set impassive countenance, severely correct in every feature, and young Mat Weatherstone, sulky because he had to ride with his grandmother now and then. He was not a nice young man.

* * * *

Diantha found it hard to write her home letters, especially to Ross. She could not tell them of all she meant to do; and she must tell them of this part of it, at once, before they heard of it through others.

To leave home—to leave school-teaching, to leave love—and "go out to service" did not seem a step up, that was certain. But she set her red lips tighter and wrote the letters; wrote them and mailed them that evening, tired though she was.

Three letters came back quickly.

Her mother's answer was affectionate, patient, and trustful, though not understanding.

Her sister's was as unpleasant as she had expected.

"The *idea!*" wrote Mrs. Susie. "A girl with a good home to live in and another to look forward to—and able to earn money *respectably!* to go out and work like a common Irish girl! Why Gerald is so mortified he can't face his friends—and I'm as ashamed as I can be! My own sister! You must be *crazy*—simply *crazy!*"

It was hard on them. Diantha had faced her own difficulties bravely enough; and sympathized keenly with her mother, and with Ross; but she had not quite visualized the mortification of her relatives. She found tears in her eyes over her mother's letter. Her sister's made her both sorry and angry—a most disagreeable feeling—as when you step on the cat on the stairs. Ross's letter she held some time without opening.

She was in her little upstairs room in the evening. She had swept, scoured, scalded and carbolized it, and the hospitally smell was now giving way to the soft richness of the outer air. The "hoo! hoo!" of the little mourning owl came to her ears through the whispering night, and large moths beat noiselessly against the window screen. She kissed the letter again, held it tightly to her heart for a moment, and opened it.

"Dearest: I have your letter with its—somewhat surprising—news. It is a comfort to know where you are, that you are settled and in no danger.

"I can readily imagine that this is but the preliminary to something else, as you say so repeatedly; and I can understand also that you are too wise to tell me all you mean to be beforehand.

"I will be perfectly frank with you, Dear.

"In the first place I love you. I shall love you always, whatever you do. But I will not disguise from you that this whole business seems to me unutterably foolish and wrong.

"I suppose you expect by some mysterious process to "develope" and "elevate" this housework business; and to make money. I should not love you any better if you made a million—and I would not take money from you—you know that, I hope. If in the years we must wait before we can marry, you are happier away from me—working in strange kitchens—or offices—that is your affair.

"I shall not argue nor plead with you, Dear Girl; I know you think you are doing right; and I have no right, nor power, to prevent you. But if my wish were right and power, you would be here to-night, under the shadow of the acacia boughs—in my arms!

"Any time you feel like coming back you will be welcome, Dear.

"Yours, Ross."

"Any time she felt like coming back?

Diantha slipped down in a little heap by the bed, her face on the letter—her arms spread wide. The letter grew wetter and wetter, and her shoulders shook from time to time.

But the hands were tight-clenched, and if you had been near enough you might have heard a dogged repetition, monotonous as a Tibetan prayer mill: "It is right. It is right. It is right." And then. "Help me—please! I need it." Diantha was not "gifted in prayer."

When Mr. Porne came home that night he found the wifely smile which is supposed to greet all returning husbands quite genuinely in evidence. "O Edgar!" cried she in a triumphant whisper, "I've got such a nice girl! She's just as neat and quick; you've no idea the work she's done today—it looks like another place already. But if things look queer at dinner don't notice it—for I've just given her her head. I was so tired, and baby bothered so, and she said that perhaps she could manage all by herself if I was willing to risk it, so I took baby for a car-ride and have only just got back. And I *think* the dinner's going to be lovely!"

It was lovely. The dining-room was cool and flyless. The table was set with an assured touch. A few of Orchardina's ever ready roses in a glass bowl gave an air of intended beauty Mrs. Porne had had no time for.

The food was well-cooked and well-served, and the attendance showed an intelligent appreciation of when people want things and how they want them.

Mrs. Porne quite glowed with exultation, but her husband gently suggested that the newness of the broom was visibly uppermost, and that such palpable perfections were probably accompanied by some drawbacks. But he liked her looks, he admitted, and the cooking would cover a multitude of sins.

On this they rested, while the week went by. It was a full week, and a short one. Mrs. Porne, making hay while the sun shone, caught up a little in her sewing and made some conscience-tormenting calls.

When Thursday night came around she was simply running over with information to give her husband.

"Such a talk as I have had with Miss Bell! She is so queer! But she's nice too, and it's all reasonable enough, what she says. You know she's studied this thing all out, and she knows about it—statistics and things. I was astonished till I found she used to teach school. Just think of it! And to be willing to work out! She certainly does her work beautiful, but—it doesn't seem like having a servant at all. I feel as if I—boarded with her!"

"Why she seemed to me very modest and unpresuming," put in Mr. Porne.

"O yes, she never presumes. But I mean the capable way she manages—I don't have to tell her one thing, nor to oversee, nor criticize. I spoke of it and she said, 'If I didn't understand the business I should have no right to undertake it.'"

"That's a new point of view, isn't it?" asked her husband. "Don't they usually make you teach them their trade and charge for the privilege?"

"Yes, of course they do. But then she does have her disadvantages—as you said."

"Does she? What are they?"

"Why she's so—rigid. I'll read you her—I don't know what to call it. She's written out a definite proposition as to her staying with us, and I want you to study it, it's the queerest thing I ever saw."

The document was somewhat novel. A clear statement of the hours of labor required in the position, the quality and amount of the different kinds of work; the terms on which she was willing to undertake it, and all prefaced by a few remarks on the status of household labor which made Mr. Porne open his eyes.

Thus Miss Bell; "The ordinary rate for labor in this state,

unskilled labor of the ordinary sort, is $2.00 a day. This is in return for the simplest exertion of brute force, under constant supervision and direction, and involving no serious risk to the employer."

"Household labor calls for the practice of several distinct crafts, and, to be properly done, requires thorough training and experience. Its performer is not only in a position of confidence, as necessarily entrusted with the care of the employer's goods and with knowledge of the most intimate family relations; but the work itself, in maintaining the life and health of the members of the household, is of most vital importance.

"In consideration of existing economic conditions, however, I am willing to undertake these intricate and responsible duties for a seven day week at less wages than are given the street-digger, for $1.50 a day."

"Good gracious, my dear!" said Mr. Porne, laying down the paper, "This young woman does appreciate her business! And we're to be let off easy at $45.00 a month, are we."

"And feel under obligations at that!" answered his wife. "But you read ahead. It is most instructive. We shall have to ask her to read a paper for the Club!"

"'In further consideration of the conditions of the time, I am willing to accept part payment in board and lodging instead of cash. Such accommodations as are usually offered with this position may be rated at $17.00 a month.'"

"O come now, don't we board her any better than that?"

"That's what I thought, and I asked her about it, and she explained that she could get a room as good for a dollar and a-half a week—she had actually made inquiries in this very town! And she could; really a better room, better furnished, that is, and service with it. You know I've always meant to get the girl's room fixed more prettily, but usually they don't seem to mind. And as to food—you see she knows all about the cost of things, and the materials she consumes are really not more than two dollars and a half a week, if they are that. She even made some figures for me to prove it—see."

Mr. Porne had to laugh.

"Breakfast. Coffee at thirty-five cents per pound, one cup, one cent. Oatmeal at fourteen cents per package, one bowl, one cent. Bread at five cents per loaf, two slices, one-half cent. Butter at forty cents per pound, one piece, one and a-half cents. Oranges at thirty cents per dozen, one, three cents. Milk at eight cents per quart, on oatmeal, one cent. Meat or fish or egg, average five cents. Total—thirteen cents."

"There! And she showed me dinner and lunch the same way. I had no idea food, just the material, cost so little. It's the labor, she says that makes it cost even in the cheapest restaurant."

"I see," said Mr. Porne. "And in the case of the domestic servant we furnish the materials and she furnishes the labor. She cooks her own food and waits on herself—naturally it wouldn't come high. What does she make it?"

```
'Food, average per day.........................$0.35
Room, $1.50 per w'k, ave. per day................  .22
                                                  _____
                                                   $.57

Total, per month............................ $17.10

$1.50 per day, per month ....................$45.00
```

"'Remaining payable in cash, $28.00.' Do I still live! But my dear Ellie, that's only what an ordinary first-class cook charges, out here, without all this fuss!"

"I know it, Ned, but you know we think it's awful, and we're always telling about their getting their board and lodging clear—as if we gave'em that out of the goodness of our hearts!"

"Exactly, my dear. And this amazing and arithmetical young woman makes us feel as if we were giving her wampum instead of money—mere primitive barter of ancient days in return for her twentieth century services! How does she do her work—that's the main question."

"I never saw anyone do it better, or quicker, or easier. That is, I thought it was easy till she brought me this paper. Just read about her work, and you'll feel as if we ought to pay her all your salary."

Mr. Porne read:

Labor performed, average ten hours a day, as follows: Preparation of food materials, care of fires, cooking, table service, and cleaning of dishes, utensils, towels, stove, etc., per meal—breakfast two hours, dinner three hours, supper or lunch one hour—six hours per day for food service. Daily chamber work and dusting, etc., one and one-half hours per day. Weekly cleaning for house of nine rooms, with halls, stairs, closets, porches, steps, walks, etc., sweeping, dusting, washing windows, mopping, scouring, etc., averaging two hours per day. Door service, waiting on tradesmen, and extras one-half hour per day. Total ten hours per day.

"That sounds well. Does it take that much time every day?"

"Yes, indeed! It would take me twenty!" she answered. "You know the week I was here alone I never did half she does. Of course I had Baby, but then I didn't do the things. I guess when it doesn't take so long they just don't do what ought to be done. For she is quick, awfully quick about her work. And she's thorough. I suppose it ought to be done that way—but I never had one before."

"She keeps mighty fresh and bright-looking after these herculean labors."

"Yes, but then she rests! Her ten hours are from six-thirty a.m., when she goes into the kitchen as regularly as a cuckoo clock, to eight-thirty p.m. when she is all through and her kitchen looks like a—well it's as clean and orderly as if no one was ever in it."

"Ten hours—that's fourteen."

"I know it, but she takes out four. She claims time to eat her meals."

"Preposterous!"

"Half an hour apiece, and half an hour in the morning to rest—and two in the afternoon. Anyway she is out, two hours every afternoon, riding in the electric cars!"

"That don't look like a very hard job. Her day laborer doesn't get two hours off every afternoon to take excursions into the country!"

"No, I know that, but he doesn't begin so early, nor stop so late. She does her square ten hours work, and I suppose one has a right to time off."

"You seem dubious about that, my dear."

"Yes, that's just where it's awkward. I'm used to girls being in all the time, excepting their day out. You see I can't leave baby, nor always take him—and it interferes with my freedom afternoons."

"Well—can't you arrange with her somehow?"

"See if you can. She says she will only give ten hours of time for a dollar and a half a day—tisn't but fifteen cents an hour—I have to pay a woman twenty that comes in. And if she is to give up her chance of sunlight and fresh air she wants me to pay her extra—by the hour. Or she says, if I prefer, she would take four hours every other day—and so be at home half the time. I said it was difficult to arrange—with baby, and she was very sympathetic and nice, but she won't alter her plans."

"Let her go, and get a less exacting servant."

"But—she does her work so well! And it saves a lot, really. She knows all about marketing and things, and plans the meals so as to have things lap, and it's a comfort to have her in the house and feel so safe and sure everything will be done right."

"Well, it's your province, my dear. I don't profess to advise. But I assure you I appreciate the table, and the cleanness of everything, and the rested look in your eyes, dear girl!"

She slipped her hand into his affectionately. "It does make a difference," she said. "I *could* get a girl for $20.00 and save nearly $2.60 a week—but you know what they are!"

"I do indeed," he admitted fervently. "It's worth the money to have this thing done so well. I think she's right about the wages. Better keep her."

"O—she'll only agree to stay six months even at this rate!"

"Well—keep her six months and be thankful. I thought she was too good to last!"

They looked over the offered contract again. It closed with:

> This agreement to hold for six months from date if mutually satisfactory. In case of disagreement two weeks' notice is to be given on either side, or two weeks' wages if preferred by the employer." It was dated, and signed "Miss D. C. Bell."

And with inward amusement and great display of penmanship they added "Mrs. Isabel J. Porne," and the contract was made.

CHAPTER VI: THE CYNOSURE

It's a singular thing that the commonest place
Is the hardest to properly fill;
That the labor imposed on a full half the race
Is so seldom performed with good will—
To say nothing of knowledge or skill!

What we ask of all women, we stare at in one,
And tribute of wonderment bring;
If this task of the million is once fitly done
We all hold our hands up and sing!
It's really a singular thing!

Isabel Porne was a cautious woman, and made no acclaim over her new acquisition until its value was proven. Her husband also bided his time; and when congratulated on his improved appearance and air of contentment, merely vouchsafed that his wife had a new girl who could cook.

To himself he boasted that he had a new wife who could love—so cheerful and gay grew Mrs. Porne in the changed atmosphere of her home.

"It is remarkable, Edgar," she said, dilating repeatedly on the peculiar quality of their good fortune. "It's not only good cooking, and good waiting, and a clean house—cleaner than I ever saw one before; and it's not only the quietness, and regularity and economy—why the bills have gone down more than a third!"

"Yes—even I noticed that," he agreed.

"But what I enjoy the most is the *atmosphere*," she continued. "When I have to do the work, the house is a perfect nightmare to me!" She leaned forward from her low stool, her elbows on her knees, her chin in her hands, and regarded him intently.

"Edgar! You know I love you. And I love my baby—I'm no unfeeling monster! But I can tell you frankly that if I'd had any idea of what housework was like I'd never have given up architecture to try it."

"Lucky for me you hadn't!" said he fondly. "I know it's been hard for you, little girl. I never meant that you should give up architecture—that's a business a woman could carry on at home I thought, the designing part anyway. There's your 'drawing-room' and all your things—"

"Yes," she said, with reminiscent bitterness, "there they are—and there they might have stayed, untouched—if Miss Bell hadn't come!"

"Makes you call her "Miss Bell" all the time, does she?"

Mrs. Porne laughed. "Yes. I hated it at first, but she asked if I could give her any real reason why the cook should be called by her first name more than the seamstress or governess. I tried to say that it was shorter, but she smiled and said that in this case it was longer!—Her name is Diantha—I've seen it on letters. And it is one syllable longer. Anyhow I've got used to Miss Bell now."

"She gets letters often?"

"Yes—very often—from Topolaya where she came from. I'm afraid she's engaged." Mrs. Porne sighed ruefully.

"I don't doubt it!" said Mr. Porne. "That would account for her six months' arrangement! Well, my dear—make hay while the sun shines!"

"I do!" she boasted. "Whole stacks! I've had a seamstress in, and got all my clothes in order and the baby's. We've had lot of dinner-parties and teas as you know—all my "social obligations" are cleared off! We've had your mother for a visit, and mine's coming now—and I wasn't afraid to have either of them! There's no fault to be found with my housekeeping now! And there are two things better than that—yes, three."

"The best thing is to see you look so young and handsome and happy again," said her husband, with a kiss.

"Yes—that's one. Another is that now I feel so easy and lighthearted I can love you and baby—as—as I *do!* Only when I'm tired and discouraged I can't put my hand on it somehow."

He nodded sympathetically. "I know, dear," he said. "I feel that way myself—sometimes. What's the other?"

"Why that's best of all!" she cried triumphantly. "I can Work again! When Baby's asleep I get hours at a time; and even when he's awake I've fixed a place where he can play—and I can draw and plan—just as I used to—*better* than I used to!"

"And that is even more to you than loving?" he asked in a quiet inquiring voice.

"It's more because it means *both!*" She leaned to him, glowing, "Don't you see? First I had the work and loved it. Then you came—and I loved you—better! Then Baby came and I loved him—best? I don't know—you and baby are all one somehow."

There was a brief interim and then she drew back, blushing richly. "Now stop—I want to explain. When the housework got to be such a nightmare—and I looked forward to a whole lifetime of it and *no* improvement; then I just *ached* for my work—and couldn't do it! And then—why sometimes dear, I just wanted to run away! Actually! From *both* of you!—you see,

I spent five years studying—I was a *real* architect—and it did hurt to see it go. And now—O now I've got It and You too, darling! *And* the Baby!—O I'm so happy!"

"Thanks to the Providential Miss Bell," said he. "If she'll stay I'll pay her anything!"

The months went by.

Peace, order, comfort, cleanliness and economy reigned in the Porne household, and the lady of the house blossomed into richer beauty and happiness; her contentment marred only by a sense of flying time.

Miss Bell fulfilled her carefully specified engagement to the letter; rested her peaceful hour in the morning; walked and rode in the afternoon; familiarized herself with the length and breadth of the town; and visited continuously among the servants of the neighborhood, establishing a large and friendly acquaintance. If she wore rubber gloves about the rough work, she paid for them herself; and she washed and ironed her simple and pretty costumes herself—with the result that they stayed pretty for surprising periods.

She wrote letters long and loving, to Ross daily; to her mother twice a week; and by the help of her sister's authority succeeded in maintaining a fairly competent servant in her deserted place.

"Father was bound he wouldn't," her sister wrote her; "but I stood right up to him, I can now I'm married!—and Gerald too—that he'd no right to take it out of mother even if he was mad with you. He made a fuss about your paying for the girl—but that was only showing off—*he* couldn't pay for her just now—that's certain. And she does very well—a good strong girl, and quite devoted to mother." And then she scolded furiously about her sister's "working out."

Diantha knew just how hard it was for her mother. She had faced all sides of the question before deciding.

"Your mother misses you badly, of course," Ross wrote her. "I go in as often as I can and cheer her up a bit. It's not just the work—she misses you. By the way—so do I." He expressed his views on her new employment.

Diantha used to cry over her letters quite often. But she would put them away, dry her eyes, and work on at the plans she was maturing, with grim courage. "It's hard on them now," she would say to herself. "Its hard on me—some. But we'll all be better off because of it, and not only us—but everybody!"

Meanwhile the happy and unhappy households of the fair town buzzed in comment and grew green with envy.

In social circles and church circles and club circles, as also in domestic circles, it was noised abroad that Mrs. Edgar Porne had "solved the servant question." News of this marvel of efficiency and propriety was discussed in every household, and not only so but in barber-shops and other downtown meeting places mentioned. Servants gathered it at dinner-tables; and Diantha, much amused, regathered it from her new friends among the servants.

"Does she keep on just the same?" asked little Mrs. Ree of Mrs. Porne in an awed whisper.

"Just the same if not better. I don't even order the meals now, unless I want something especial. She keeps a calendar of what we've had to eat, and what belongs to the time of year, prices and things. When I used to ask her to suggest (one does, you know: it is so hard to think up a variety!), she'd always be ready with an idea, or remind me that we had had so and so two days before, till I asked her if she'd like to order, and she said she'd be willing to try, and now I just sit down to the table without knowing what's going to be there."

"But I should think that would interfere with your sense of freedom," said Mrs. Ellen A Dankshire, "A woman should be mistress of her own household."

"Why I am! I order whenever I specially want anything. But she really does it more—more scientifically. She has made a study of it. And the bills are very much lower."

"Well, I think you are the luckiest woman alive!" sighed Mrs. Ree. "I wish I had her!"

Many a woman wished she had her, and some, calling when they knew Mrs. Porne was out, or descending into their own kitchens of an evening when the strange Miss Bell was visiting "the help," made flattering propositions to her to come to them. She was perfectly polite and agreeable in manner, but refused all blandishments.

"What are you getting at your present place—if I may ask?" loftily inquired the great Mrs. Thaddler, ponderous and beaded.

"There is surely no objection to your asking, madam," she replied politely. "Mrs. Porne will not mind telling you, I am sure."

"Hm!" said the patronizing visitor, regarding her through her lorgnette. "Very good. Whatever it is I'll double it. When can you come?"

"My engagement with Mrs. Porne is for six months," Diantha answered, "and I do not wish to close with anyone else until that time is up. Thank you for your offer just the same."

"Peculiarly offensive young person!" said Mrs. Thaddler to her husband. "Looks to me like one of these literary imposters. Mrs. Porne will probably appear in the magazines before long."

Mr. Thaddler instantly conceived a liking for the young person, "sight unseen."

Diantha acquired quite a list of offers; places open to her as soon as she was free; at prices from her present seven dollars up to the proposed doubling.

"Fourteen dollars a week and found!—that's not so bad," she meditated. "That would mean over $650 clear in a year! It's a wonder to me girls don't try it long enough to get a start at something else. With even two or three hundred ahead—and an outfit—it would be easier to make good in a store or any other way. Well—I have other fish to fry!"

So she pursued her way; and, with Mrs. Porne's permission— held a sort of girl's club in her spotless kitchen one evening a week during the last three months of her engagement. It was a "Study and Amusement Club." She gave them short and interesting lessons in arithmetic, in simple dressmaking, in easy and thorough methods of housework. She gave them lists of books, referred them to articles in magazines, insidiously taught them to use the Public Library.

They played pleasant games in the second hour, and grew well acquainted. To the eye or ear of any casual visitor it was the simplest and most natural affair, calculated to "elevate labor" and to make home happy.

Diantha studied and observed. They brought her their poor confidences, painfully similar. Always poverty—or they would not be there. Always ignorance, or they would not stay there. Then either incompetence in the work, or inability to hold their little earnings—or both; and further the Tale of the Other Side— the exactions and restrictions of the untrained mistresses they served; cases of withheld wages; cases of endless requirements; cases of most arbitrary interference with their receiving friends and "followers," or going out; and cases, common enough to be horrible, of insult they could only escape by leaving.

"It's no wages, of course—and no recommendation, when you leave like that—but what else can a girl do, if she's honest?"

So Diantha learned, made friends and laid broad foundations.

The excellence of her cocking was known to many, thanks to the weekly "entertainments." No one refused. No one regretted acceptance. Never had Mrs. Porne enjoyed such a sense of social importance.

All the people she ever knew called on her afresh, and people she never knew called on her even more freshly. Not that she was directly responsible for it. She had not triumphed cruelly over her less happy friends; nor had she cried aloud on the street corners concerning her good fortune. It was not her fault, nor, in truth anyone's. But in a community where the "servant question" is even more vexed than in the country at large, where the local product is quite unequal to the demand, and where distance makes importation an expensive matter, the fact of one woman's having, as it appeared, settled this vexed question, was enough to give her prominence.

Mrs. Ellen A. Dankshire, President of the Orchardina Home and Culture Club, took up the matter seriously.

"Now Mrs. Porne," said she, settling herself vigorously into a comfortable chair, "I just want to talk the matter over with you, with a view to the club. We do not know how long this will last—"

"Don't speak of it!" said Mrs. Porne.

"—and it behooves us to study the facts while we have them."

"So much is involved!" said little Mrs. Ree, the Corresponding Secretary, lifting her pale earnest face with the perplexed fine lines in it. "We are all so truly convinced of the sacredness of the home duties!"

"Well, what do you want me to do?" asked their hostess.

"We must have that remarkable young woman address our club!" Mrs. Dankshire announced. "It is one case in a thousand, and must be studied!"

"So noble of her!" said Mrs. Ree. "You say she was really a school-teacher? Mrs. Thaddler has put it about that she is one of these dreadful writing persons—in disguise!"

"O no," said Mrs. Porne. "She is perfectly straightforward about it, and had the best of recommendations. She was a teacher, but it didn't agree with her health, I believe."

"Perhaps there is a story to it!" Mrs. Ree advanced; but Mrs. Dankshire disagreed with her flatly.

"The young woman has a theory, I believe, and she is working it out. I respect her for it. Now what we want to ask you, Mrs. Porne, is this: do you think it would make any trouble for you—in the household relations, you know—if we ask her to read a paper to the Club? Of course we do not wish to interfere, but it is a remarkable opportunity—very. You know the fine work Miss Lucy Salmon has done on this subject; and Miss Frances Kellor. You know how little data we have, and how great, how serious, a question it is daily becoming! Now here is a young woman of brains and culture who has apparently grappled with the question; her example and influence must not be lost! We must hear from her. The public must know of this."

"Such an ennobling example!" murmured Mrs. Ree. "It might lead numbers of other school-teachers to see the higher side of the home duties!"

"Furthermore," pursued Mrs. Dankshire, "this has occured to me. Would it not be well to have our ladies bring with them to the meeting the more intelligent of their servants; that they might hear and see the—the dignity of household labor—so ably set forth?

"Isn't it—wouldn't that be a—an almost dangerous experiment?" urged Mrs. Ree; her high narrow forehead fairly creped with little wrinkles: "She might—say something, you know, that they might—take advantage of!"

"Nonsense, my dear!" replied Mrs. Dankshire. She was very fond of Mrs. Ree, but had small respect for her judgment. "What could she say? Look at what she does! And how beautifully—how perfectly—she does it! I would wager now—*may* I try an experiment Mrs. Porne?" and she stood up, taking out her handkerchief.

"Certainly," said Mrs. Porne, "with pleasure! You won't find any!"

Mrs. Dankshire climbed heavily upon a carefully selected chair and passed her large clean plain-hemmed handkerchief across the top of a picture.

"I knew it!" she proclaimed proudly from her eminence, and showed the cloth still white. "That," she continued in ponderous descent, "that is Knowledge, Ability and Conscience!"

"I don't see how she gets the time!" breathed Mrs. Ree, shaking her head in awed amazement, and reflecting that she would not dare trust Mrs. Dankshire's handkerchief on her picture tops.

"We must have her address the Club," the president repeated. "It will do worlds of good. Let me see—a paper on—we might say 'On the True Nature of Domestic Industry.' How does that strike you, Mrs. Ree?"

"Admirable!" said Mrs. Ree. "So strong! so succinct."

"That certainly covers the subject," said Mrs. Porne. "Why don't you ask her?"

"We will. We have come for that purpose. But we felt it right to ask you about it first," said Mrs. Dankshire.

"Why I have no control over Miss Bell's movements, outside of working hours," answered Mrs. Porne. "And I don't see that it would make any difference to our relations. She is a very self-poised young woman, but extremely easy to get along with. And I'm sure she could write a splendid paper. You'd better ask her, I think."

"Would you call her in?" asked Mrs. Dankshire, "or shall we go out to the kitchen?"

"Come right out; I'd like you to see how beautifully she keeps everything."

The kitchen was as clean as the parlor; and as prettily arranged. Miss Bell was making her preparation for lunch, and stopped to receive the visitors with a serenely civil air—as of a country store-keeper.

"I am very glad to meet you, Miss Bell, very glad indeed," said Mrs. Dankshire, shaking hands with her warmly. "We have at heard so much of your beautiful work here, and we admire your attitude! Now would you be willing to give a paper—or a talk—to our club, the Home and Culture Club, some Wednesday, on The True Nature of Domestic Industry?"

Mrs. Ree took Miss Bell's hand with something of the air of a Boston maiden accosting a saint from Hindoostan. "If you only would!" she said. "I am sure it would shed light on this great subject!"

Miss Bell smiled at them both and looked at Mrs. Porne inquiringly.

"I should be delighted to have you do it," said her employer. "I know it would be very useful."

"Is there any date set?" asked Miss Bell.

"Any Wednesday after February," said Mrs. Dankshire.

"Well—I will come on the first Wednesday in April. If anything should happen to prevent I will let you know in good season, and if you should wish to postpone or alter the program—should think better of the idea—just send me word. I shall not mind in the least."

They went away quite jubilant, Miss Bell's acceptance was announced officially at the next club-meeting, and the Home and Culture Club felt that it was fulfilling its mission.

CHAPTER VII: HERESY AND SCHISM

You may talk about religion with a free and open mind,
For ten dollars you may criticize a judge;
You may discuss in politics the newest thing you find,
And open scientific truth to all the deaf and blind,
But there's one place where the brain must never
budge!

CHORUS.

Oh, the Home is Utterly Perfect!
And all its works within!
To say a word about it—
To criticize or doubt it—
To seek to mend or move it—
To venture to improve it—
Is The Unpardonable Sin!
　　　　　　　—"Old Song."

Mr. Porne took an afternoon off and came with his wife to hear their former housemaid lecture. As many other men as were able did the same. All the members not bedridden were present, and nearly all the guests they had invited.

So many were the acceptances that a downtown hall had been taken; the floor was more than filled, and in the gallery sat a block of servant girls, more gorgeous in array than the ladies below whispering excitedly among themselves. The platform recalled a "tournament of roses," and, sternly important among all that fragrant loveliness, sat Mrs. Dankshire in "the chair" flanked by Miss Torbus, the Recording Secretary, Miss Massing, the Treasurer, and Mrs. Ree, tremulous with importance in her official position. All these ladies wore an air of high emprise, even more intense than that with which they usually essayed their public duties. They were richly dressed, except Miss Torbus, who came as near it as she could.

At the side, and somewhat in the rear of the President, on a chair quite different from "the chair," discreetly gowned and of a bafflingly serene demeanor, sat Miss Bell. All eyes were upon her—even some opera glasses.

"She's a good-looker anyhow," was one masculine opinion.

"She's a peach," was another, "Tell you—the chap that gets her is well heeled!" said a third.

The ladies bent their hats toward one another and conferred in flowing whispers; and in the gallery eager confidences were exchanged, with giggles.

On the small table before Mrs. Dankshire, shaded by a magnificent bunch of roses, lay that core and crux of all parliamentry dignity, the gavel; an instrument no self-respecting chairwoman may be without; yet which she still approaches with respectful uncertainty.

In spite of its large size and high social standing, the Orchardina Home and Culture Club contained some elements of unrest, and when the yearly election of officers came round there was always need for careful work in practical politics to keep the reins of government in the hands of "the right people."

Mrs. Thaddler, conscious of her New York millions, and Madam Weatherstone, conscious of her Philadelphia lineage, with Mrs. Johnston A. Marrow ("one of the Boston Marrows!" was awesomely whispered of her), were the heads of what might be called "the conservative party" in this small parliament; while Miss Miranda L. Eagerson, describing herself as 'a journalist,' who held her place in local society largely by virtue of the tacit dread of what she might do if offended—led the more radical element.

Most of the members were quite content to follow the lead of the solidly established ladies of Orchard Avenue; especially as this leadership consisted mainly in the pursuance of a masterly inactivity. When wealth and aristocracy combine with that common inertia which we dignify as "conservatism" they exert a powerful influence in the great art of sitting still.

Nevertheless there were many alert and conscientious women in this large membership, and when Miss Eagerson held the floor, and urged upon the club some active assistance in the march of events, it needed all Mrs. Dankshire's generalship to keep them content with marking time.

On this auspicious occasion, however, both sides were agreed in interest and approval. Here was a subject appealing to every woman present, and every man but such few as merely "boarded"; even they had memories and hopes concerning this question.

Solemnly rose Mrs. Dankshire, her full silks rustling about her, and let one clear tap of the gavel fall into the sea of soft whispering and guttural murmurs.

In the silence that followed she uttered the momentous announcements: "The meeting will please come to order," "We will now hear the reading of the minutes of the last meeting," and so on most conscientiously through officer's reports and committees reports to "new business."

Perhaps it is their more frequent practice of religious rites, perhaps their devout acceptance of social rulings and the dictates of fashion, perhaps the lifelong reiterance of small duties at home, or all these things together, which makes women so seriously letter-perfect in parliamentry usage. But these stately ceremonies were ended in course of time, and Mrs. Dankshire rose again, even more solemn than before, and came forward majestically.

"Members—and guests," she said impressively, "this is an occasion which brings pride to the heart of every member of the Home and Culture Club. As our name implies, this Club is formed to serve the interests of The Home—those interests which stand first, I trust, in every human heart."

A telling pause, and the light patter of gloved hands.

"Its second purpose," pursued the speaker, with that measured delivery which showed that her custom, as one member put it, was to "first write and then commit," "is to promote the cause of Culture in this community. Our aim is Culture in the broadest sense, not only in the curricula of institutions of learning, not only in those spreading branches of study and research which tempts us on from height to height"—("proof of arboreal ancestry that," Miss Eagerson confided to a friend, whose choked giggle attracted condemning eyes)—"but in the more intimate fields of daily experience."

"Most of us, however widely interested in the higher education, are still—and find in this our highest honor—wives and mothers." These novel titles called forth another round of applause.

"As such," continued Mrs. Dankshire, "we all recognize the difficult—the well-nigh insuperable problems of the"—she glanced at the gallery now paying awed attention—"domestic question."

"We know how on the one hand our homes yawn unattended"—("I yawn while I'm attending—eh?" one gentleman in the rear suggested to his neighbor)—"while on the other the ranks of mercenary labor are overcrowded. Why is it that while the peace and beauty, the security and comfort, of a good home, with easy labor and high pay, are open to every young woman, whose circumstances oblige her to toil for her living, she blindly refuses these true advantages and loses her health and too often what is far more precious!—in the din and tumult of the factory, or the dangerous exposure of the public counter."

Madam Weatherstone was much impressed at this point, and beat her black fan upon her black glove emphatically. Mrs. Thaddler also nodded; which meant a good deal from her. The applause was most gratifying to the speaker, who continued:

"Fortunately for the world there are some women yet who appreciate the true values of life." A faint blush crept slowly up the face of Diantha, but her expression was unchanged. Whoso had met and managed a roomful of merciless children can easily face a woman's club.

"We have with us on this occasion one, as we my say, our equal in birth and breeding,"—Madam Weatherstone here looked painfully shocked as also did the Boston Marrow; possibly Mrs. Dankshire, whose parents were Iowa farmers, was not unmindful of this, but she went on smoothly, "and whose first employment was the honored task of the teacher; who has deliberately cast her lot with the domestic worker, and brought her trained intelligence to bear upon the solution of this great question—The True Nature of Domestic Service. In the interests of this problem she has consented to address us—I take pleasure in introducing Miss Diantha Bell."

Diantha rose calmly, stepped forward, bowed to the President and officers, and to the audience. She stood quietly for a moment, regarding the faces before her, and produced a typewritten paper. It was clear, short, and to some minds convincing.

She set forth that the term "domestic industry" did not define certain kinds of labor, but a stage of labor; that all labor was originally domestic; but that most kinds had now become social, as with weaving and spinning, for instance, for centuries confined to the home and done by women only; now done in mills by men and women; that this process of socialization has now been taken from the home almost all the manufactures—as of wine, beer, soap, candles, pickles and other specialties, and part of the laundry work; that the other processes of cleaning are also being socialized, as by the vacuum cleaners, the professional window-washers, rug cleaners, and similar professional workers; and that even in the preparation of food many kinds are now specialized, as by the baker and confectioner. That in service itself we were now able to hire by the hour or day skilled workers necessarily above the level of the "general."

A growing rustle of disapproval began to make itself felt, which increased as she went on to explain how the position of the housemaid is a survival of the ancient status of woman slavery, the family with the male head and the group of servile women.

"The keynote of all our difficulty in this relation is that we demand celibacy of our domestic servants," said Diantha.

A murmur arose at this statement, but she continued calmly:

"Since it is natural for women to marry, the result is that our domestic servants consist of a constantly changing series of young girls, apprentices, as it were; and the complicated and important duties of the household cannot be fully mastered by such hands."

The audience disapproved somewhat of this, but more of what followed. She showed (Mrs. Porne nodding her head amusedly), that so far from being highly paid and easy labor, house service was exacting and responsible, involving a high degree of skill as well as moral character, and that it was paid less than ordinary unskilled labor, part of this payment being primitive barter.

Then, as whispers and sporadic little spurts of angry talk increased, the clear quiet voice went on to state that this last matter, the position of a strange young girl in our homes, was of itself a source of much of the difficulty of the situation.

"We speak of giving them the safety and shelter of the home,"—here Diantha grew solemn;—"So far from sharing our homes, she gives up her own, and has none of ours, but the poorest of our food and a cramped lodging; she has neither the freedom nor the privileges of a home; and as to shelter and safety—the domestic worker, owing to her peculiarly defence-less position, furnishes a terrible percentage of the unfortunate."

A shocked silence met this statement.

"In England shop-workers complain of the old custom of 'sleeping in'—their employers furnishing them with lodging as part payment; this also is a survival of the old apprentice method. With us, only the domestic servant is held to this anti-quated position."

Regardless of the chill displeasure about her she cheerfully pursued:

"Let us now consider the economic side of the question.

'Domestic economy' is a favorite phrase. As a matter of fact our method of domestic service is inordinately wasteful. Even where the wife does all the housework, without pay, we still waste labor to an enormous extent, requiring one whole woman to wait upon each man. If the man hires one or more servants, the wastes increase. If one hundred men undertake some common business, they do not divide in two halves, each man having another man to serve him—fifty productive laborers, and fifty cooks. Two or three cooks could provide for the whole group; to use fifty is to waste 47 per cent. of the labor.

"But our waste of labor is as nothing to our waste of money. For, say twenty families, we have twenty kitchens with all their furnishings, twenty stoves with all their fuel; twenty cooks with all their wages; in cash and barter combined we pay about ten dollars a week for our cooks—$200 a week to pay for the cooking for twenty families, for about a hundred persons!

"Three expert cooks, one at $20 a week and two at $15 would save to those twenty families $150 a week and give them better food. The cost of kitchen furnishings and fuel, could be reduced by nine-tenths; and beyond all that comes our incredible waste in individual purchasing. What twenty families spend on individual patronage of small retailers, could be reduced by more than half if bought by competent persons in wholesale quantities. Moreover, our whole food supply would rise in quality as well as lower in price if it was bought by experts.

"To what does all this lead?" asked Diantha pleasantly.

Nobody said anything, but the visible attitude of the house seemed to say that it led straight to perdition.

"The solution for which so many are looking is no new scheme of any sort; and in particular it is not that oft repeated fore-doomed failure called 'co-operative housekeeping'."

At this a wave of relief spread perceptibly. The irritation roused by those preposterous figures and accusations was somewhat allayed. Hope was relit in darkened countenances.

"The inefficiency of a dozen tottering households is not removed by combining them," said Diantha. This was of dubious import. "Why should we expect a group of families to "keep house" expertly and economically together, when they are driven into companionship by the fact that none of them can do it alone."

Again an uncertain reception.

"Every family is a distinct unit," the girl continued. "Its needs are separate and should be met separately. The separate house and garden should belong to each family, the freedom and group privacy of the common milkman, by a common baker, by a common cooking and a common cleaning establishment. We are rapidly approaching an improved system of living in which the private home will no more want a cookshop on the premises than a blacksmith's shop or soap-factory. The necessary work of the kitchenless house will be done by the hour, with skilled labor; and we shall order our food cooked instead of raw. This will give to the employees a respectable well-paid profession, with their own homes and families; and to the employers a saving of about two-thirds of the expense of living, as well as an end of all our difficulties with the servant question. That is the way to elevate—to enoble domestic service. It must cease to be domestic service—and become world service."

Suddenly and quietly she sat down.

Miss Eagerson was on her feet. So were others.

"Madam President! Madam President!" resounded from several points at once. Madam Weatherstone—Mrs. Thaddler—no! yes—they really were both on their feet. Applause was going on—irregularly—soon dropped. Only, from the group in the gallery it was whole-hearted and consistent.

Mrs. Dankshire, who had been growing red and redder as the paper advanced, who had conferred in alarmed whispers with Mrs. Ree, and Miss Massing, who had even been seen to extend her hand to the gavel and finger it threateningly, now rose, somewhat precipitately, and came forward.

"Order, please! You will please keep order. You have heard the—we will now—the meeting is now open for discussion, Mrs. Thaddler!" And she sat down. She meant to have said

Madam Weatherstone, by Mrs. Thaddler was more aggressive.

"I wish to say," said that much beaded lady in a loud voice, "that I was against this—unfortunate experiment—from the first. And I trust it will never be repeated!" She sat down.

Two tight little dimples flickered for an instant about the corners of Diantha's mouth.

"Madam Weatherstone?" said the President, placatingly.

Madam Weatherstone arose, rather sulkily, and looked about her. An agitated assembly met her eye, buzzing universally each to each.

"Order!" said Mrs. Dankshire, "*order*, please!" and rapped three times with the gavel.

"I have attended many meetings, in many clubs, in many states," said Madam Weatherstone, "and have heard much that was foolish, and some things that were dangerous. But I will say that never in the course of all my experience have I heard anything so foolish and so dangerous, as this. I trust that the— doubtless well meant—attempt to throw light on this subject— from the wrong quarter—has been a lesson to us all. No club could survive more than one such lamentable mistake!" And she sat down, gathering her large satin wrap about her like a retiring Caesar.

"Madam President!" broke forth Miss Eagerson. "I was up first—and have been standing ever since—"

"One moment, Miss Eagerson," said Mrs. Dankshire superbly, "The Rev. Dr. Eltwood."

If Mrs. Dankshire supposed she was still further supporting the cause of condemnation she made a painful mistake. The cloth and the fine bearing of the young clergyman deceived her; and she forgot that he was said to be "advanced" and was new to the place.

"Will you come to the platform, Dr. Eltwood?"

Dr. Eltwood came to the platform with the easy air of one to whom platforms belonged by right.

"Ladies," he began in tones of cordial good will, "both employer and employed!—and gentlemen—whom I am delighted to see here to-day! I am grateful for the opportunity so graciously extended to me"—he bowed six feet of black broadcloth toward Mrs. Dankshire—"by your honored President.

"And I am grateful for the opportunity previously enjoyed, of listening to the most rational, practical, wise, true and hopeful words I have ever heard on this subject. I trust there will be enough open-minded women—and men—in Orchardina to make possible among us that higher business development of a great art which has been so convincingly laid before us. This club is deserving of all thanks from the community for extending to so many the privilege of listening to our valued fellow-citizen—Miss Bell."

He bowed again—to Miss Bell—and to Mrs. Dankshire, and resumed his seat, Miss Eagerson taking advantage of the dazed pause to occupy the platform herself.

"Mr. Eltwood is right!" she said. "Miss Bell is right! This is the true presentation of the subject, 'by one who knows.' Miss Bell has pricked our pretty bubble so thoroughly that we don't know where we're standing—but she knows! Housework is a business—like any other business—I've always said so, and it's got to be done in a business way. Now I for one—" but Miss Eagerson was rapped down by the Presidential gavel; as Mrs. Thaddler, portentous and severe, stalked forward.

"It is not my habit to make public speeches," she began, "nor my desire; but this is a time when prompt and decisive action needs to be taken. This Club cannot afford to countenance any such farrago of mischievous nonsense as we have heard to-day. I move you, Madam President, that a resolution of condemnation be passed at once; and the meeting then dismissed!"

She stalked back again, while Mrs. Marrow of Boston, in clear, cold tones seconded the motion.

But another voice was heard—for the first time in that assembly—Mrs. Weatherstone, the pretty, delicate widower daughter-in-law of Madam Weatherstone, was on her feet with

"Madam President! I wish to speak to this motion."

"Won't you come to the platform, Mrs. Weatherstone?" asked Mrs. Dankshire graciously, and the little lady came, visibly trembling, but holding her head high.

All sat silent, all expected—what was not forthcoming.

"I wish to protest, as a member of the Club, and as a woman, against the gross discourtesy which has been offered to the guest and speaker of the day. In answer to our invitation Miss Bell has given us a scholarly and interesting paper, and I move that we extend her a vote of thanks."

"I second the motion," came from all quarters.

"There is another motion before the house," from others.

Cries of "Madam President" arose everywhere, many speakers were on their feet. Mrs. Dankshire tapped frantically with the little gavel, but Miss Eagerson, by sheer vocal power, took and held the floor.

"I move that we take a vote on this question," she cried in piercing tones. "Let every woman who knows enough to appreciate Miss Bell's paper—and has any sense of decency—stand up!"

Quite a large proportion of the audience stood up—very informally. Those who did not, did not mean to acknowledge lack of intelligence and sense of decency, but to express emphatic disapproval of Miss Eagerson, Miss Bell and their views.

"I move you, Madam President," cried Mrs. Thaddler, at the top of her voice, "that every member who is guilty of such grossly unparlimentary conduct be hereby dropped from this Club!"

"We hereby resign!" cried Miss Eagerson. "*We* drop *you!* We'll have a New Woman's Club in Orchardina with some warmth in its heart and some brains in its head—even if it hasn't as much money in its pocket!"

Amid stern rappings, hissings, cries of "Order—order," and frantic "Motions to adjourn" the meeting broke up; the club elements dissolving and reforming into two bodies as by some swift chemical reaction.

Great was the rejoicing of the daily press; some amusement was felt, though courteously suppressed by the men present, and by many not present, when they heard of it.

Some ladies were so shocked and grieved as to withdraw from club-life altogether. Others, in stern dignity, upheld the shaken standards of Home and Culture; while the most conspicuous outcome of it all was the immediate formation of the New Woman's Club of Orchardina.

CHAPTER VIII

Behind the straight purple backs and smooth purple legs on the box before them, Madam Weatherstone and Mrs. Weatherstone rolled home silently, a silence of thunderous portent. Another purple person opened the door for them, and when Madam Weatherstone said, "We will have tea on the terrace," it was brought them by a fourth.

"I was astonished at your attitude, Viva," began the old lady, at length. "Of course it was Mrs. Dankshire's fault in the first place, but to encourage that,—outrageous person! How could you do it!"

Young Mrs. Weatherstone emptied her exquisite cup and set it down.

"A sudden access of courage, I suppose," she said. "I was astonished at myself."

"I wholly disagree with you!" replied her mother-in-law. "Never in my life have I heard such nonsense. Talk like that would be dangerous, if it were not absurd! It would destroy the home! It would strike at the roots of the family."

Viva eyed her quietly, trying to bear in mind the weight of a tradition, the habits of a lifetime, the effect of long years of uninterrupted worship of household gods.

"It doesn't seem so to me," she said slowly, "I was much interested and impressed. She is evidently a young woman of knowledge and experience, and put her case well. It has quite waked me up."

"It has quite upset you!" was the reply. "You'll be ill after this, I am sure. Hadn't you better go and lie down now? I'll have some dinner sent to you."

"Thank you," said Viva, rising and walking to the edge of the broad terrace. "You are very kind. No. I do not wish to lie down. I haven't felt so thoroughly awake in—" she drew a pink cluster of oleander against her cheek and thought a moment— "in several years." There was a new look about her certainly.

"Nervous excitement," her mother-in-law replied. "You're not like yourself at all to-night. You'll certainly be ill to-morrow!"

Viva turned at this and again astonished the old lady by serenely kissing her. "Not at all!" she said gaily. "I'm going to be well to-morrow. You will see!"

She went to her room, drew a chair to the wide west window with the far off view and sat herself down to think. Diantha's assured poise, her clear reasoning, her courage, her common sense; and something of tenderness and consecration she discerned also, had touched deep chords in this woman's nature. It was like the sound of far doors opening, windows thrown up, the jingle of bridles and clatter of hoofs, keen bugle notes. A sense of hope, of power, of new enthusiasm, rose in her.

Orchardina Society, eagerly observing "young Mrs. Weatherstone" from her first appearance, had always classified her as "delicate." Beside the firm features and high color of the matron-in-office, this pale quiet slender woman looked like a meek and transient visitor. But her white forehead was broad under its soft-hanging eaves of hair, and her chin, though lacking in prognathous prominence or bull-dog breadth, had a certain depth which gave hope to the physiognomist.

She was strangely roused and stirred by the afternoon's events. "I'm like that man in 'Phantastes'," she thought contemptuously, "who stayed so long in that dungeon because it didn't occur to him to open the door! Why don't I—?" she rose and walked slowly up and down, her hands behind her. "I will!" she said at last.

Then she dressed for dinner, revolving in her mind certain suspicions long suppressed, but now flaming out in clear conviction in the light of Diantha's words. "Sleeping in, indeed!" she murmured to herself. "And nobody doing anything!"

She looked herself in the eye in the long mirror. Her gown was an impressive one, her hair coiled high, a gold band ringed it like a crown. A clear red lit her checks.

She rang. Little Ilda, the newest maid, appeared, gazing at her in shy admiration. Mrs. Weatherstone looked at her with new eyes. "Have you been here long?" she asked. "What is your name?"

"No, ma'am," said the child—she was scarce more. "Only a week and two days. My name is Ilda."

"Who engaged you?"

"Mrs. Halsey, ma'am."

"Ah," said Mrs. Weatherstone, musing to herself, "and I engaged Mrs. Halsey!" "Do you like it here?" she continued kindly.

"Oh yes, ma'am!" said Ilda. "That is—" she stopped, blushed, and continued bravely. "I like to work for you, ma'am."

"Thank you, Ilda. Will you ask Mrs. Halsey to come to me—at once, please."

Ilda went, more impressed than ever with the desirability of her new place, and mistress.

As she was about to pass the door of Mr. Matthew Weatherstone, that young gentleman stepped out and intercepted her. "Whither away so fast, my dear?" he amiably inquired.

"Please let one pass, sir! I'm on an errand. Please, sir?"

"You must give me a kiss first!" said he—and since there seemed no escape and she was in haste, she submitted. He took six—and she ran away half crying.

Mrs. Halsey, little accustomed to take orders from her real mistress, and resting comfortably in her room, had half a mind to send an excuse.

"I'm not dressed," she said to the maid.

"Well she is!" replied Ilda, "dressed splendid. She said 'at once, please.'"

"A pretty time o' day!" said the housekeeper with some asperity, hastily buttoning her gown; and she presently appeared, somewhat heated, before Mrs. Weatherstone.

That lady was sitting, cool and gracious, her long ivory paper-cutter between the pages of a new magazine.

"In how short a time could you pack, Mrs. Halsey?" she inquired.

"Pack, ma'am? I'm not accustomed to doing packing. I'll send one of the maids. Is it your things, ma'am?"

"No," said Mrs. Weatherstone. "It is yours I refer to. I wish you to pack your things and leave the house—in an hour. One of the maids can help you, if necessary. Anything you cannot take can be sent after you. Here is a check for the following month's wages."

Mrs. Halsey was nearly a head taller than her employer, a stout showy woman, handsome enough, red-lipped, and with a moist and crafty eye. This was so sudden a misadventure that she forgot her usual caution. "You've no right to turn me off in a minute like this!" she burst forth. "I'll leave it to Madam Weatherstone!"

"If you will look at the terms on which I engaged you, Mrs. Halsey, you will find that a month's warning, or a month's wages, was specified. Here are the wages—as to the warning, that has been given for some months past!"

"By whom, Ma'am?"

"By yourself, Mrs. Halsey—I think you understand me. Oscar will take your things as soon as they are ready."

Mrs. Halsey met her steady eye a moment—saw more than she cared to face—and left the room.

She took care, however, to carry some letters to Madam Weatherstone, and meekly announced her discharge; also, by some coincidence, she met Mr. Matthew in the hall upstairs, and weepingly confided her grievance to him, meeting immediate consolation, both sentimental and practical.

When hurried servants were sent to find their young

mistress they reported that she must have gone out, and in truth she had; out on her own roof, where she sat quite still, though shivering a little now and then from the new excitement, until dinner time.

This meal, in the mind of Madam Weatherstone, was the crowning factor of daily life; and, on state occasions, of social life. In her cosmogony the central sun was a round mahogany table; all other details of housekeeping revolved about it in varying orbits. To serve an endless series of dignified delicious meals, notably dinners, was, in her eyes, the chief end of woman; the most high purpose of the home.

Therefore, though angry and astounded, she appeared promptly when the meal was announced; and when her daughter-in-law, serene and royally attired, took her place as usual, no emotion was allowed to appear before the purple footman who attended.

"I understood you were out, Viva," she said politely.

"I was," replied Viva, with equal decorum. "It is charming outside at this time in the evening—don't you think so?"

Young Matthew was gloomy and irritable throughout the length and breadth of the meal; and when they were left with their coffee in the drawing room, he broke out, "What's this I hear about Mrs. Halsey being fired without notice?"

"That is what I wish to know, Viva," said the grandmother. "The poor woman is greatly distressed. Is there not some mistake?"

"It's a damn shame," said Matthew.

The younger lady glanced from one to the other, and wondered to see how little she minded it. "The door was there all the time!" she thought to herself, as she looked her stepson in the eye and said, "Hardly drawing-room language, Matthew. Your grandmother is present!"

He stared at her in dumb amazement, so she went on, "No, there is no mistake at all. I discharged Mrs. Halsey about an hour before dinner. The terms of the engagement were a month's warning or a month's wages. I gave her the wages."

"But! but!" Madam Weatherstone was genuinely confused by this sudden inexplicable, yet perfectly polite piece of what she still felt to be in the nature of 'interference' and 'presumption.' "I have had no fault to find with her."

"I have, you see," said her daughter-in-law smiling. "I found her unsatisfactory and shall replace her with something better presently. How about a little music, Matthew? Won't you start the victrolla?"

Matthew wouldn't. He was going out; went out with the word. Madam Weatherstone didn't wish to hear it—had a headache—must go to her room—went to her room forthwith. There was a tension in the atmosphere that would have wrung tears from Viva Weatherstone a week ago, yes, twenty-four hours ago.

As it was she rose to her feet, stretching herself to her full height, and walked the length of the great empty room. She even laughed a little. "It's open!" said she, and ordered the car. While waiting for it she chatted with Mrs. Porne awhile over the all-convenient telephone.

* * * *

Diantha sat at her window, watching the big soft, brilliant moon behind the eucalyptus trees. After the close of the strenuous meeting, she had withdrawn from the crowd of excited women anxious to shake her hand and engage her on the spot, had asked time to consider a number of good opportunities offered, and had survived the cold and angry glances of the now smaller but far more united Home and Culture Club. She declined to talk to the reporters, and took refuge first in an open car. This proved very unsatisfactory, owing to her sudden prominence. Two persistent newspaper men swung themselves upon the car also and insisted on addressing her.

"Excuse me, gentlemen," she said, "I am not acquainted with you."

They eagerly produced their cards—and said they were "newspaper men."

"I see," said Diantha, "But you are still men? And gentlemen,

I suppose? I am a woman, and I do not wish to talk with you."

"Miss Bell Declines to Be Interviewed," wrote the reporters, and spent themselves on her personal appearance, being favorably impressed thereby.

But Miss Bell got off at the next corner and took a short cut to the house where she had rented a room. Reporters were waiting there, two being women.

Diantha politely but firmly declined to see them and started for the stairs; but they merely stood in front of her and asked questions. The girl's blood surged to her cheeks; she smiled grimly, kept absolute silence, brushed through them and went swiftly to her room, locking the door after her.

The reporters described her appearance—unfavorably this time; and they described the house—also unfavorably. They said that "A group of adoring-eyed young men stood about the doorway as the flushed heroine of the afternoon made her brusque entrance." These adorers consisted of the landlady's Johnny, aged thirteen, and two satellites of his, still younger. They *did* look at Diantha admiringly; and she *was* a little hurried in her entrance—truth must be maintained.

Too irritated and tired to go out for dinner, she ate an orange or two, lay down awhile, and then eased her mind by writing a long letter to Ross and telling him all about it. That is, she told him most of it, all the pleasant things, all the funny things; leaving out about the reporters, because she was too angry to be just, she told herself. She wrote and wrote, becoming peaceful as the quiet moments passed, and a sense grew upon her of the strong, lasting love that was waiting so patiently.

"Dearest," her swift pen flew along, "I really feel much encouraged. An impression has been made. One or two men spoke to me afterward; the young minister, who said such nice things; and one older man, who looked prosperous and reliable. 'When you begin any such business as you have outlined, you may count on me, Miss Bell,' he said, and gave me his card. He's a lawyer—P. L. Wiscomb; nice man, I should think. Another big, sheepish-looking man said, 'And me, Miss Bell.' His name is Thaddler; his wife is very disagreeable. Some of the women are favorably impressed, but the old-fashioned kind—my! 'If hate killed men, Brother Lawrence!'—but it don't."

She wrote herself into a good humor, and dwelt at considerable length on the pleasant episode of the minister and young Mrs. Weatherstone's remarks. "I liked her," she wrote. "She's a nice woman—even if she is rich."

There was a knock at her door. "Lady to see you, Miss."

"I cannot see anyone," said Diantha; "you must excuse me."

"Beg pardon, Miss, but it's not a reporter; it's—" The landlady stretched her lean neck around the door edge and whispered hoarsely, "It's young Mrs. Weatherstone!"

Diantha rose to her feet, a little bewildered. "I'll be right down," she said. But a voice broke in from the hall, "I beg your pardon, Miss Bell, but I took the liberty of coming up; may I come in?"

She came in, and the landlady perforce went out. Mrs. Weatherstone held Diantha's hand warmly, and looked into her eyes. "I was a schoolmate of Ellen Porne," she told the girl. "We are dear friends still; and so I feel that I know you better than you think. You have done beautiful work for Mrs. Porne; now I want you to do to it for me. I need you."

"Won't you sit down?" said Diantha.

"You, too," said Mrs. Weatherstone. "Now I want you to come to me—right away. You have done me so much good already. I was just a New England bred school teacher myself at first, so we're even that far. Then you took a step up—and I took a step down."

Diantha was a little slow in understanding the quick fervor of this new friend; a trifle suspicious, even; being a cautious soul, and somewhat overstrung, perhaps. Her visitor, bright-eyed and eager, went on. "I gave up school teaching and married a fortune. You have given it up to do a more needed work. I think you are wonderful. Now, I know this seems queer to you, but I want to tell you about it. I feel sure you'll understand. At home, Madam Weatherstone has had everything in charge for years and years, and I've been too lazy or too weak, or too indifferent, to do anything. I didn't care, somehow. All the machinery of living, and no *living*—no good of it all! Yet there didn't seem to be anything else to do. Now you have waked me all up—your paper this afternoon—what Mr. Eltwood said—the way those poor, dull, blind women took it. And yet I was just as dull and blind myself! Well, I begin to see things now. I can't tell you all at once what a difference it has made; but I have a very definite proposition to make to you. Will you come and be my housekeeper, now—right away—at a hundred dollars a month?"

Diantha opened her eyes wide and looked at the eager lady as if she suspected her nervous balance.

"The other one got a thousand a year—you are worth more. Now, don't decline, please. Let me tell you about it. I can see that you have plans ahead, for this business; but it can't hurt you much to put them off six months, say. Meantime, you could be practicing. Our place at Santa Ulrica is almost as big as this one; there are lots of servants and a great, weary maze of accounts to be kept, and it wouldn't be bad practice for you—now, would it?"

Diantha's troubled eyes lit up. "No—you are right there," she said. "If I could do it!"

"You'll have to do just that sort of thing when you are running your business, won't you?" her visitor went on. "And the summer's not a good time to start a thing like that, is it?"

Diantha meditated. "No, I wasn't going to. I was going to start somewhere—take a cottage, a dozen girls or so—and furnish labor by the day to the other cottages."

"Well, you might be able to run that on the side," said Mrs. Weatherstone. "And you could train my girls, get in new ones if you like; it doesn't seem to me it would conflict. But to speak to you quite frankly, Miss Bell, I want you in the house for my own sake. You do me good."

They discussed the matter for some time, Diantha objecting mainly to the suddenness of it all. "I'm a slow thinker," she said, "and this is so—so attractive that I'm suspicious of it. I had the other thing all planned—the girls practically engaged."

"Where were you thinking of going?" asked Mrs. Weatherstone.

"To Santa Ulrica."

"Exactly! Well, you shall have your cottage and our girls and give them part time. Or—how many have you arranged with?"

"Only six have made definite engagements yet."

"What kind?"

"Two laundresses, a cook and three second maids; all good ones."

"Excellent! Now, I tell you what to do. I will engage all those girls. I'm making a change at the house, for various reasons. You bring them to me as soon as you like; but you I want at once. I wish you'd come home with me to-night! Why don't you?"

Diantha's scanty baggage was all in sight. She looked around for an excuse. Mrs. Weatherstone stood up laughing.

"Put the new address in the letter," she said, mischievously, "and come along!"

* * * *

And the purple chauffeur, his disapproving back ineffectual in the darkness, rolled them home.

CHAPTER IX: "SLEEPING IN"

Men have marched in armies, fleets have borne them,
Left their homes new countries to subdue;
Young men seeking fortune wide have wandered—
We have something new.

Armies of young maidens cross our oceans;
Leave their mother's love, their father's care;
Maidens, young and helpless, widely wander,
Burdens new to bear.

Strange the land and language, laws and customs;
Ignorant and all alone they come;
Maidens young and helpless, serving strangers,
Thus we keep the Home.

When on earth was safety for young maidens
Far from mother's love and father's care?
We preserve The Home, and call it sacred—
Burdens new they bear.

The sun had gone down on Madam Weatherstone's wrath, and risen to find it unabated. With condensed disapprobation written on every well-cut feature, she came to the coldly gleaming breakfast table.

That Mrs. Halsey was undoubtedly gone, she had to admit; yet so far failed to find the exact words of reproof for a woman of independent means discharging her own housekeeper when it pleased her.

Young Mathew unexpectedly appeared at breakfast, perhaps in anticipation of a sort of Roman holiday in which his usually late and apologetic stepmother would furnish the amusement. They were both surprised to find her there before them, looking uncommonly fresh in crisp, sheer white, with deep-toned violets in her belt.

She ate with every appearance of enjoyment, chatting amiably about the lovely morning—the flowers, the garden and the gardeners; her efforts ill seconded, however.

"Shall I attend to the orders this morning?" asked Madam Weatherstone with an air of noble patience.

"O no, thank you!" replied Viva. "I have engaged a new

housekeeper."

"A new housekeeper! When?" The old lady was shaken by this inconceivable promptness.

"Last night," said her daughter-in-law, looking calmly across the table, her color rising a little.

"And when is she coming, if I may ask?"

"She has come. I have been with her an hour already this morning."

Young Mathew smiled. This was amusing, though not what he had expected. "How extremely alert and businesslike!" he said lazily. "It's becoming to you—to get up early!"

"You can't have got much of a person—at a minute's notice," said his grandmother. "Or perhaps you have been planning this for some time?"

"No," said Viva. "I have wanted to get rid of Mrs. Halsey for some time, but the new one I found yesterday."

"What's her name?" inquired Mathew.

"Bell—Miss Diantha Bell," she answered, looking as calm as if announcing the day of the week, but inwardly dreading the result somewhat. Like most of such terrors it was overestimated.

There was a little pause—rather an intense little pause; and then—"Isn't that the girl who set 'em all by the ears yesterday?" asked the young man, pointing to the morning paper. "They say she's a good-looker."

Madam Weatherstone rose from the table in some agitation. "I must say I am very sorry, Viva, that you should have been so— precipitate! This young woman cannot be competent to manage a house like this—to say nothing of her scandalous ideas. Mrs. Halsey was—to my mind—perfectly satisfactory. I shall miss her very much." She swept out with an unanswerable air.

"So shall I," muttered Mat, under his breath, as he strolled after her; "unless the new one's equally amiable."

Viva Weatherstone watched them go, and stood awhile looking after the well-built, well-dressed, well-mannered but far from well-behaved young man.

"I don't *know*," she said to herself, "but I do feel—think—

imagine—a good deal. I'm sure I hope not! Anyway—it's new life to have that girl in the house."

That girl had undertaken what she described to Ross as "a large order—a very large order."

"It's the hardest thing I ever undertook," she wrote him, "but I think I can do it; and it will be a tremendous help. Mrs. Weatherstone's a brick—a perfect brick! She seems to have been very unhappy—for ever so long—and to have submitted to her domineering old mother-in-law just because she didn't care enough to resist. Now she's got waked up all of a sudden— she says it was my paper at the club—more likely my awful example, I think! and she fired her old housekeeper—I don't know what for—and rushed me in.

"So here I am. The salary is good, the work is excellent training, and I guess I can hold the place. But the old lady is a terror, and the young man—how you would despise that Johnny!"

The home letters she now received were rather amusing. Ross, sternly patient, saw little difference in her position. "I hope you will enjoy your new work," he wrote, "but personally I should prefer that you did not—so you might give it up and come home sooner. I miss you as you can well imagine. Even when you were here life was hard enough—but now!!!!!!

"I had a half offer for the store the other day, but it fell through. If I could sell that incubus and put the money into a ranch—fruit, hens, anything—then we could all live on it; more cheaply, I think; and I could find time for some research work I have in mind. You remember that guinea-pig experiment I want so to try?"

Diantha remembered and smiled sadly. She was not much interested in guinea-pigs and their potential capacities, but she was interested in her lover and his happiness. "Ranch," she said thoughtfully; "that's not a bad idea."

Her mother wrote the same patient loving letters, perfunctorily hopeful. Her father wrote none—"A woman's business—this letter-writin'," he always held; and George, after one scornful upbraiding, had "washed his hands of her" with some sense of relief. He didn't like to write letters either.

But Susie kept up a lively correspondence. She was attached to her sister, as to all her immediate relatives and surroundings; and while she utterly disapproved of Diantha's undertaking, a sense of sisterly duty, to say nothing of affection, prompted her to many letters. It did not, however, always make these agreeable reading.

"Mother's pretty well, and the girl she's got now does nicely—that first one turned out to be a failure. Father's as cranky as ever. We are all well here and the baby (this was a brand new baby Diantha had not seen) is just a Darling! You ought to be here, you unnatural Aunt! Gerald doesn't ever speak of you—but I do just the same. You hear from the Wardens, of course. Mrs. Warden's got neuralgia or something; keeps them all busy. They are much excited over this new place of yours—you ought to hear them go on! It appears that Madam Weatherstone is a connection of theirs—one of the F. F. V's, I guess, and they think she's something wonderful. And to have *you* working *there!*—well, you can just see how they'd feel; and I don't blame them. It's no use arguing with you—but I should think you'd have enough of this disgraceful foolishness by this time and come home!"

Diantha tried to be very philosophic over her home letters; but they were far from stimulating. "It's no use arguing with poor Susie!" she decided. "Susie thinks the sun rises and sets between kitchen, nursery and parlor!

"Mother can't see the good of it yet, but she will later— Mother's all right.

"I'm awfully sorry the Wardens feel so—and make Ross unhappy—but of course I knew they would. It can't be helped. It's just a question of time and work."

And she went to work.

* * * *

Mrs. Porne called on her friend most promptly, with a natural eagerness and curiosity.

"How does it work? Do you like her as much as you thought? Do tell me about it, Viva. You look like another woman already!"

"I certainly feel like one," Viva answered. "I've seen slaves in housework, and I've seen what we fondly call 'Queens' in housework; but I never saw brains in it before."

Mrs. Porne sighed. "Isn't it just wonderful—the way she does things! Dear me! We do miss her! She trained that Swede for us—and she does pretty well—but not like 'Miss Bell'! I wish there were a hundred of her!"

"If there were a hundred thousand she wouldn't go round!" answered Mrs. Weatherstone. "How selfish we are! *That* is the kind of woman we all want in our homes—and fuss because we can't have them."

"Edgar says he quite agrees with her views," Mrs. Porne went on. "Skilled labor by the day ... food sent in ... He says if she cooked it he wouldn't care if it came all the way from Alaska! She certainly can cook! I wish she'd set up her business—the sooner the better."

Mrs. Weatherstone nodded her head firmly. "She will. She's planning. This was really an interruption—her coming here, but I think it will be a help—she's not had experience in large management before, but she takes hold splendidly. She's found a dozen 'leaks' in our household already."

"Mrs. Thaddler's simply furious, I hear," said the visitor. "Mrs. Ree was in this morning and told me all about it. Poor Mrs. Ree! The home is church and state to her; that paper of Miss Bell's she regards as simple blasphemy."

They both laughed as that stormy meeting rose before them.

"I was so proud of you, Viva, standing up for her as you did. How did you ever dare?"

"Why I got my courage from the girl herself. She was—superb! Talk of blasphemy! Why I've committed *lese majeste* and regicide and the Unpardonable Sin since that meeting!" And she told her friend of her brief passage at arms with Mrs.

Halsey. "I never liked the woman," she continued; "and some of the things Miss Bell said set me thinking. I don't believe we half know what's going on in our houses."

"Well, Mrs. Thaddler's so outraged by 'this scandalous attack upon the sanctities of the home' that she's going about saying all sorts of things about Miss Bell. O look—I do believe that's her car!"

Even as they spoke a toneless voice announced, "Mr. and Mrs. Thaddler," and Madam Weatherstone presently appeared to greet these visitors.

"I think you are trying a dangerous experiment!" said Mrs. Thaddler to her young hostess. "A very dangerous experiment! Bringing that young iconoclast into your home!"

Mr. Thaddler, stout and sulky, sat as far away as he could and talked to Mrs. Porne. "I'd like to try that same experiment myself," said he to her. "You tried it some time, I understand?"

"Indeed we did—and would still if we had the chance," she replied. "We think her a very exceptional young woman."

Mr. Thaddler chuckled. "She is that!" he agreed. "Gad! How she did set things humming! They're humming yet—at our house!"

He glanced rather rancorously at his wife, and Mrs. Porne wished, as she often had before, that Mr. Thaddler wore more clothing over his domestic afflictions.

"Scandalous!" Mrs. Thaddler was saying to Madam Weatherstone. "Simply scandalous! Never in my life did I hear such absurd—such outrageous—charges against the sanctities of the home!"

"There you have it!" said Mr. Thaddler, under his breath. "Sanctity of the fiddlesticks! There was a lot of truth in what that girl said!" Then he looked rather sheepish and flushed a little—which was needless; easing his collar with a fat finger.

Madam Weatherstone and Mrs. Thaddler were at one on this subject; but found it hard to agree even so, no love being lost between them; and the former gave evidence of more satisfaction than distress at this "dangerous experiment" in the house of her friends. Viva sat silent, but with a look of watchful intelligence that delighted Mrs. Porne.

"It has done her good already," she said to herself. "Bless that girl!"

Mr. Thaddler went home disappointed in the real object of his call—he had hoped to see the Dangerous Experiment again. But his wife was well pleased.

"They will rue it!" she announced. "Madam Weatherstone is ashamed of her daughter-in-law—I can see that! *She* looks cool enough. I don't know what's got into her!"

"Some of that young woman's good cooking," her husband suggested.

"That young woman is not there as cook!" she replied tartly. "What she *is* there for we shall see later! Mark my words!"

Mr. Thaddler chuckled softly. "I'll mark 'em!" he said.

Diantha had her hands full. Needless to say her sudden entrance was resented by the corps of servants accustomed to the old regime. She had the keys; she explored, studied, inventoried, examined the accounts, worked out careful tables and estimates. "I wish Mother were here!" she said to herself. "She's a regular genius for accounts. I *can* do it—but it's no joke."

She brought the results to her employer at the end of the week. "This is tentative," she said, "and I've allowed margins because I'm new to a business of this size. But here's what this house ought to cost you—at the outside, and here's what it does cost you now."

Mrs. Weatherstone was impressed. "Aren't you a little—spectacular?" she suggested.

Diantha went over it carefully; the number of rooms, the number of servants, the hours of labor, the amount of food and other supplies required.

"This is only preparatory, of course," she said. "I'll have to check it off each month. If I may do the ordering and keep all the accounts I can show you exactly in a month, or two at most."

"How about the servants?" asked Mrs. Weatherstone.

There was much to say here, questions of competence, of impertinence, of personal excellence with "incompatibility of temper." Diantha was given a free hand, with full liberty to experiment, and met the opportunity with her usual energy.

She soon discharged the unsatisfactory ones, and substituted the girls she had selected for her summer's experiment, gradually adding others, till the household was fairly harmonious, and far more efficient and economical. A few changes were made among the men also.

By the time the family moved down to Santa Ulrica, there was quite a new spirit in the household. Mrs. Weatherstone fully approved of the Girls' Club Diantha had started at Mrs. Porne's; and it went on merrily in the larger quarters of the great "cottage" on the cliff.

"I'm very glad I came to you, Mrs. Weatherstone," said the girl. "You were quite right about the experience; I did need it— and I'm getting it!"

She was getting some of which she made no mention.

As she won and held the confidence of her subordinates, and the growing list of club members, she learned their personal stories; what had befallen them in other families, and what they liked and disliked in their present places.

"The men are not so bad," explained Catharine Kelly, at a club meeting, meaning the men servants; "they respect an honest girl if she respects herself; but it's the young masters—and sometimes the old ones!"

"It's all nonsense," protested Mrs. James, widowed cook of long standing. "I've worked out for twenty-five years, and I never met no such goings on!"

Little Ilda looked at Mrs. James' severe face and giggled.

"I've heard of it," said Molly Connors, "I've a cousin that's workin' in New York; and she's had to leave two good places on account of their misbehavin' theirselves. She's a fine girl, but too good-lookin'."

Diantha studied types, questioned them, drew them out, adjusted facts to theories and theories to facts. She found the weakness of the whole position to lie in the utter ignorance and helplessness of the individual servant. "If they were only organized," she thought—"and knew their own power!—Well; there's plenty of time."

As her acquaintance increased, and as Mrs. Weatherstone's interest in her plans increased also, she started the small summer experiment she had planned, for furnishing labor by the day. Mrs. James was an excellent cook, though most unpleasant to work with. She was quite able to see that getting up frequent lunches at three dollars, and dinners at five dollars, made a better income than ten dollars a week even with several days unoccupied.

A group of younger women, under Diantha's sympathetic encouragement, agreed to take a small cottage together, with Mrs. James as a species of chaperone; and to go out in twos and threes as chambermaids and waitresses at 25 cents an hour. Two of them could set in perfect order one of the small beach cottage in an hour's time; and the occupants, already crowded for room, were quite willing to pay a little more in cash "not to have a servant around." Most of them took their meals out in any case.

It was a modest attempt, elastic and easily alterable and based on the special conditions of a shore resort: Mrs. Weatherstone's known interest gave it social backing; and many ladies who heartily disapproved of Diantha's theories found themselves quite willing to profit by this very practical local solution of the "servant question."

The "club girls" became very popular. Across the deep hot sand they ploughed, and clattered along the warping boardwalks, in merry pairs and groups, finding the work far more varied and amusing than the endless repetition in one household. They had pleasant evenings too, with plenty of callers, albeit somewhat checked and chilled by rigorous Mrs. James.

"It is both foolish and wicked!" said Madam Weatherstone to her daughter-in-law, "Exposing a group of silly girls to such danger and temptations! I understand there is singing and laughing going on at that house until half-past ten at night."

"Yes, there is," Viva admitted. "Mrs. James insists that they shall all be in bed at eleven—which is very wise. I'm glad they have good times—there's safety in numbers, you know."

"There will be a scandal in this community before long!" said the old lady solemnly. "And it grieves me to think that this household will be responsible for it!"

Diantha heard all this from the linen room while Madam Weatherstone buttonholed her daughter-in-law in the hall; and in truth the old lady meant that she should hear what she said.

"She's right, I'm afraid!" said Diantha to herself—"there will be a scandal if I'm not mighty careful and this household will be responsible for it!"

Even as she spoke she caught Ilda's childish giggle in the lower hall, and looking over the railing saw her airily dusting the big Chinese vases and coquetting with young Mr. Mathew.

Later on, Diantha tried seriously to rouse her conscience and her common sense. "Don't you see, child, that it can't do you anything but harm? You can't carry on with a man like that as you can with one of your own friends. He is not to be trusted. One nice girl I had here simply left the place—he annoyed her so."

Ilda was a little sulky. She had been quite a queen in the small Norwegian village she was born in. Young men were young men—and they might even—perhaps! This severe young housekeeper didn't know everything. Maybe she was jealous!

So Ilda was rather unconvinced, though apparently submissive, and Diantha kept a careful eye upon her. She saw to it that Ilda's room had a bolt as well as key in the door, and kept the room next to it empty; frequently using it herself, unknown to anyone. "I hate to turn the child off," she said to herself, conscientiously revolving the matter. "She isn't doing a thing more than most girls do—she's only a little fool. And he's not doing anything I can complain of—yet."

But she worried over it a good deal, and Mrs. Weatherstone noticed it.

"Doesn't your pet club house go well, 'Miss Bell?' You seem troubled about something."

"I am," Diantha admitted. "I believe I'll have to tell you about it—but I hate to. Perhaps if you'll come and look I shan't have to say much."

She led her to a window that looked on the garden, the rich, vivid, flower-crowded garden of Southern California by the sea. Little Ilda, in a fresh black frock and snowy, frilly cap and apron, ran out to get a rose; and while she sniffed and dallied they saw Mr. Mathew saunter out and join her.

The girl was not as severe with him as she ought to have been—that was evident; but it was also evident that she was frightened and furious when he suddenly held her fast and kissed her with much satisfaction. As soon as her arms were free she gave him a slap that sounded smartly even at that distance; and ran crying into the house.

"She's foolish, I admit," said Diantha,—"but she doesn't realize her danger at all. I've tried to make her. And now I'm more worried than ever. It seems rather hard to discharge her— she needs care."

"I'll speak to that young man myself," said Mrs. Weatherstone. "I'll speak to his grandmother too!"

"O—would you?" urged Diantha. "She wouldn't believe anything except that the girl 'led him on'—you know that. But I have an idea that we could convince her—if you're willing to do something rather melodramatic—and I think we'd better do it to-night!"

"What's that?" asked her employer; and Diantha explained. It was melodramatic, but promised to be extremely convincing.

"Do you think he'd dare! under my roof?" hotly demanded Madam Weatherstone.

"I'm very much afraid it wouldn't be the first time," Diantha reluctantly assured her. "It's no use being horrified. But if we could only make sure—"

"If we could only make his grandmother sure!" cried Madam Weatherstone. "That would save me a deal of trouble and misunderstanding. See here—I think I can manage it—what makes you think it's to-night?"

"I can't be absolutely certain—" Diantha explained; and told her the reasons she had.

"It does look so," her employer admitted. "We'll try it at any rate."

Urging her mother-in-law's presence on the ground of needing her experienced advice, Mrs. Weatherstone brought the august lady to the room next to Ilda's late that evening, the housekeeper in attendance.

"We mustn't wake the servants," she said in an elaborate whisper. "They need sleep, poor things! But I want to consult you about these communicating doors and the locksmith is coming in the morning.—you see this opens from this side." She turned the oiled key softly in the lock. "Now Miss Bell thinks they ought to be left so—so that the girls can visit one another if they like—what do you think?"

"I think you are absurd to bring me to the top floor, at this time of night, for a thing like this!" said the old lady. "They should be permanently locked, to my mind! There's no question about it."

Viva, still in low tones, discussed this point further; introduced the subject of wall-paper or hard finish; pointed out from the window a tall eucalyptus which she thought needed heading; did what she could to keep her mother-in-law on the spot; and presently her efforts were rewarded.

A sound of muffled speech came from the next room—a man's voice dimly heard. Madam Weatherstone raised her head like a warhorse.

"What's this! What's this!" she said in a fierce whisper.

Viva laid a hand on her arm. "Sh!" said she. "Let us make sure!" and she softly unlatched the door.

A brilliant moon flooded the small chamber. They could see little Ilda, huddled in the bedclothes, staring at her door from which the key had fallen. Another key was being inserted—turned—but the bolt held.

"Come and open it, young lady!" said a careful voice outside.

"Go away! Go away!" begged the girl, low and breathlessly. "Oh how *can* you! Go away quick!"

"Indeed, I won't!" said the voice. "You come and open it."

"Go away," she cried, in a soft but frantic voice. "I—I'll scream!"

"Scream away!" he answered. "I'll just say I came up to see what the screaming's about, that's all. You open the door—if you don't want anybody to know I'm here! I won't hurt you any—I just want to talk to you a minute."

Madam Weatherstone was speechless with horror, her daughter-in-law listened with set lips. Diantha looked from one to the other, and at the frightened child before them who was now close to the terrible door.

"O please!—*please!* go away!" she cried in desperation. "O what shall I do! What shall I do!"

"You can't do anything," he answered cheerfully. "And I'm coming in anyhow. You'd better keep still about this for your own sake. Stand from under!" Madam Weatherstone marched into the room. Ilda, with a little cry, fled out of it to Diantha.

There was a jump, a scramble, two knuckly hands appeared, a long leg was put through the transom, two legs wildly wriggling, a descending body, and there stood before them, flushed, dishevelled, his coat up to his ears—Mat Weatherstone.

He did not notice the stern rigidity of the figure which stood between him and the moonlight, but clasped it warmly to his heart.—"Now I've got you, Ducky!" cried he, pressing all too affectionate kisses upon the face of his grandmother.

Young Mrs. Weatherstone turned on the light.

It was an embarrassing position for the gentleman.

He had expected to find a helpless cowering girl; afraid to cry out because her case would be lost if she did; begging piteously that he would leave her; wholly at his mercy.

What he did find was so inexplicable as to reduce him to

gibbering astonishment. There stood his imposing grandmother, so overwhelmed with amazement that her trenchant sentences failed her completely; his stepmother, wearing an expression that almost suggested delight in his discomfiture; and Diantha, as grim as Rhadamanthus.

Poor little Ilda burst into wild sobs and choking explanations, clinging to Diantha's hand. "If I'd only listened to you!" she said. "You told me he was bad! I never thought he'd do such an awful thing!"

Young Mathew fumbled at the door. He had locked it outside in his efforts with the pass-key. He was red, red to his ears—very red, but there was no escape. He faced them—there was no good in facing the door.

They all stood aside and let him pass—a wordless gauntlet.

Diantha took the weeping Ilda to her room for the night. Madam Weatherstone and Mrs. Weatherstone went down together.

"She must have encouraged him!" the older lady finally burst forth.

"She did not encourage him to enter her room, as you saw and heard," said Viva with repressed intensity.

"He's only a boy!" said his grandmother.

"She is only a child, a helpless child, a foreigner, away from home, untaught, unprotected," Viva answered swiftly; adding with quiet sarcasm—"Save for the shelter of the home!"

They parted in silence.

CHAPTER X: UNION HOUSE

"We are weak!" said the Sticks, and men broke them;
We are weak!" said the Threads, and were torn;
Till new thoughts came and they spoke them;
Till the Fagot and the Rope were born.

For the Fagot men find is resistant,
And they anchor on the Rope's taut length;
Even grasshoppers combined,
Are a force, the farmers find—
In union there is strength.

Ross Warden endured his grocery business; strove with it, toiled at it, concentrated his scientific mind on alien tasks of financial calculation and practical psychology, but he liked it no better. He had no interest in business, no desire to make money, no skill in salesmanship.

But there were five mouths at home; sweet affectionate feminine mouths no doubt, but requiring food. Also two in the kitchen, wider, and requiring more food. And there were five backs at home to be covered, to use the absurd metaphor—as if all one needed for clothing was a four foot patch. The amount and quality of the covering was an unceasing surprise to Ross, and he did not do justice to the fact that his womenfolk really saved a good deal by doing their own sewing.

In his heart he longed always to be free of the whole hated load of tradesmanship. Continually his thoughts went back to the hope of selling out the business and buying a ranch.

"I could make it keep us, anyhow," he would plan to himself; "and I could get at that guinea pig idea. Or maybe hens would do." He had a theory of his own, or a personal test of his own, rather, which he wished to apply to a well known theory. It would take some years to work it out, and a great many fine pigs, and be of no possible value financially. "I'll do it some-time," he always concluded; which was cold comfort.

His real grief at losing the companionship of the girl he loved, was made more bitter by a total lack of sympathy with her aims, even if she achieved them—in which he had no confidence. He had no power to change his course, and tried not to be unpleasant about it, but he had to express his feelings now and then.

"Are you coming back to me?" he wrote. "How con you bear to give so much pain to everyone who loves you? Is your wonderful salary worth more to you than being here with your mother—with me? How can you say you love me—and ruin both our lives like this? I cannot come to see you—I *would* not come to see you—calling at the back door! Finding the girl I love in a cap and apron! Can you not see it is wrong, utterly wrong, all this mad escapade of yours? Suppose you do make a thousand dollars a year—I shall never touch your money— you know that. I cannot even offer you a home, except with my family, and I know how you feel about that; I do not blame you.

"But I am as stubborn as you are, dear girl; I will not live on my wife's money—you will not live in my mother's house—and we are drifting apart. It is not that I care less for you dear, or at all for anyone else, but this is slow death—that's all."

Mrs. Warden wrote now and then and expatiated on the sufferings of her son, and his failing strength under the unnatural strain, till Diantha grew to dread her letters more than any pain she knew. Fortunately they came seldom.

Her own family was much impressed by the thousand dollars, and found the occupation of housekeeper a long way more tolerable than that of house-maid, a distinction which made Diantha smile rather bitterly. Even her father wrote to her once, suggesting that if she chose to invest her salary according to his advice he could double it for her in a year, maybe treble it, in Belgian hares.

"They'd double and treble fast enough!" she admitted to herself; but she wrote as pleasant a letter as she could, declining his proposition.

Her mother seemed stronger, and became more sympathetic as the months passed. Large affairs always appealed to her more than small ones, and she offered valuable suggestions as to the account keeping of the big house. They all assumed that she was permanently settled in this well paid position, and she made no confidences. But all summer long she planned and read and studied out her progressive schemes, and strengthened her hold among the working women.

Laundress after laundress she studied personally and tested professionally, finding a general level of mediocrity, till finally she hit upon a melancholy Dane—a big rawboned red-faced woman—whose husband had been a miller, but was hurt about the head so that he was no longer able to earn his living. The huge fellow was docile, quiet, and endlessly strong, but needed constant supervision.

"He'll do anything you tell him, Miss, and do it well; but then he'll sit and dream about it—I can't leave him at all. But he'll take the clothes if I give him a paper with directions, and come right back." Poor Mrs. Thorald wiped her eyes, and went on with her swift ironing.

Diantha offered her the position of laundress at Union House, with two rooms for their own, over the laundry. "There'll be work for him, too," she said. "We need a man there. He can do a deal of the heavier work—be porter you know. I can't offer him very much, but it will help some."

Mrs. Thorald accepted for both, and considered Diantha as a special providence.

There was to be cook, and two capable second maids. The work of the house must be done thoroughly well, Diantha determined; "and the food's got to be good—or the girls wont stay." After much consideration she selected one Julianna, a "person of color," for her kitchen: not the jovial and sloppy personage usually figuring in this character, but a tall, angular, and somewhat cynical woman, a misanthrope in fact, with a small son. For men she had no respect whatever, but conceded a grudging admiration to Mr. Thorald as "the usefullest biddablest male person" she had ever seen. She also extended special sympathy to Mrs. Thorald on account of her peculiar burden, and the Swedish woman had no antipathy to her color, and seemed to take a melancholy pleasure in Julianna's caustic speeches.

Diantha offered her the place, boy and all. "He can be 'bell boy' and help you in the kitchen, too. Can't you, Hector?" Hector rolled large adoring eyes at her, but said nothing. His mother accepted the proposition, but without enthusiasm. "I can't keep no eye on him, Miss, if I'm cookin' an less'n you keep your eye on him they's no work to be got out'n any kind o' boy."

"What is your last name, Julianna?" Diantha asked her.

"I suppose, as a matter o' fac' its de name of de last nigger I married," she replied. "Dere was several of 'em, all havin' different names, and to tell you de truf Mis' Bell, I got clean mixed amongst 'em. But Julianna's my name—world without end amen."

So Diantha had to waive her theories about the surnames of servants in this case.

"Did they all die?" she asked with polite sympathy.

"No'm, dey didn't none of 'em die—worse luck."

"I'm afraid you have seen much trouble, Julianna," she continued sympathetically; "They deserted you, I suppose?"

Julianna laid her long spoon upon the table and stood up with great gravity. "No'm," she said again, "dey didn't none of 'em desert me on no occasion. I divorced 'em."

Marital difficulties in bulk were beyond Diantha's comprehension, and she dropped the subject.

Union House opened in the autumn. The vanished pepper trees were dim with dust in Orchardina streets as the long rainless summer drew to a close; but the social atmosphere fairly sparkled with new interest. Those who had not been away chattered eagerly with those who had, and both with the incoming tide of winter visitors.

"That girl of Mrs. Porne's has started her housekeeping shop!"

"That 'Miss Bell' has got Mrs. Weatherstone fairly infatuated with her crazy schemes."

"Do you know that Bell girl has actually taken Union House? Going to make a Girl's Club of it!"

"Did you ever *hear* of such a thing! Diantha Bell's really going to try to run her absurd undertaking right here in Orchardina!"

They did not know that the young captain of industry

had deliberately chosen Orchardina as her starting point on account of the special conditions. The even climate was favorable to "going out by the day," or the delivery of meals, the number of wealthy residents gave opportunity for catering on a large scale; the crowding tourists and health seekers made a market for all manner of transient service and cooked food, and the constant lack of sufficient or capable servants forced the people into an unwilling consideration of any plan of domestic assistance.

In a year's deliberate effort Diantha had acquainted herself with the rank and file of the town's housemaids and day workers, and picked her assistants carefully. She had studied the local conditions thoroughly, and knew her ground. A big faded building that used to be "the Hotel" in Orchardina's infant days, standing, awkward and dingy on a site too valuable for a house lot and not yet saleable as a business block, was the working base.

A half year with Mrs. Weatherstone gave her $500 in cash, besides the $100 she had saved at Mrs. Porne's; and Mrs. Weatherstone's cheerfully offered backing gave her credit.

"I hate to let you," said Diantha, "I want to do it all myself."

"You are a painfully perfect person, Miss Bell," said her last employer, pleasantly, "but you have ceased to be my housekeeper and I hope you will continue to be my friend. As a friend I claim the privilege of being disagreeable. If you have a fault it is conceit. Immovable Colossal Conceit! And Obstinacy!"

"Is that all?" asked Diantha.

"It's all I've found—so far," gaily retorted Mrs. Weatherstone. "Don't you see, child, that you can't afford to wait? You have reasons for hastening, you know. I don't doubt you could, in a series of years, work up this business all stark alone. I have every confidence in those qualities I have mentioned! But what's the use? You'll need credit for groceries and furniture. I am profoundly interested in this business. I am more than willing to advance a little capital, or to ensure your credit. A man would have sense enough to take me up at once."

"I believe you are right," Diantha reluctantly agreed. "And you shan't lose by it!"

Her friends were acutely interested in her progress, and showed it in practical ways. The New Woman's Club furnished five families of patrons for the regular service of cooked food, which soon grew, with satisfaction, to a dozen or so, varying from time to time. The many families with invalids, and lonely invalids without families, were glad to avail themselves of the special delicacies furnished at Union House. Picnickers found it easier to buy Diantha's marvelous sandwiches than to spend golden morning hours in putting up inferior ones at home; and many who cooked for themselves, or kept servants, were glad to profit by this outside source on Sunday evenings and "days out."

There was opposition too; both the natural resistance of inertia and prejudice, and the active malignity of Mrs. Thaddler.

The Pornes were sympathetic and anxious.

"That place'll cost her all of $10,000 a year, with those twenty-five to feed, and they only pay $4.50 a week—I know that!" said Mr. Porne.

"It does look impossible," his wife agreed, "but such is my faith in Diantha Bell I'd back her against Rockefeller!"

Mrs. Weatherstone was not alarmed at all. "If she *should* fail—which I don't for a moment expect—it wont ruin me," she told Isabel. "And if she succeeds, as I firmly believe she will, why, I'd be willing to risk almost anything to prove Mrs. Thaddler in the wrong."

Mrs. Thaddler was making herself rather disagreeable. She used what power she had to cry down the undertaking, and was so actively malevolent that her husband was moved to covert opposition. He never argued with his wife—she was easily ahead of him in that art, and, if it came to recriminations, had certain controvertible charges to make against him, which mode him angrily silent. He was convinced in a dim way that her ruthless domineering spirit, and the sheer malice she often showed, were more evil things than his own bad habits; and that even in their domestic relation her behavior really caused him more pain and discomfort than he caused her; but he could not convince her of it, naturally.

"That Diantha Bell is a fine girl," he said to himself. "A damn fine girl, and as straight as a string!"

There had crept out, through the quenchless leak of servants talk, a varicolored version of the incident of Mathew and the transom; and the town had grown so warm for that young gentleman that he had gone to Alaska suddenly, to cool off, as it were. His Grandmother, finding Mrs. Thaddler invincible with this new weapon, and what she had so long regarded as her home now visibly Mrs. Weatherstone's, had retired in regal dignity to her old Philadelphia establishment, where she upheld the standard of decorum against the weakening habits of a deteriorated world, for many years.

As Mr. Thaddler thought of this sweeping victory, he chuckled for the hundredth time. "She ought to make good, and she will. Something's got to be done about it," said he.

Diantha had never liked Mr. Thaddler; she did not like that kind of man in general, nor his manner toward her in particular. Moreover he was the husband of Mrs. Thaddler. She did not know that he was still the largest owner in the town's best grocery store, and when that store offered her special terms for her exclusive trade, she accepted the proposition thankfully.

She told Ross about it, as a matter well within his knowledge, if not his liking, and he was mildly interested. "I am much alarmed at this new venture," he wrote, "but you must get your experience. I wish I could save you. As to the groceries, those are wholesale rates, nearly; they'll make enough on it. Yours is a large order you see, and steady."

When she opened her "Business Men's Lunch" Mr. Thaddler had a still better opportunity. He had a reputation as a high flyer, and had really intended to sacrifice himself on the altar of friendship by patronizing and praising this "undertaking" at any cost to his palate; but no sacrifice was needed.

Diantha's group of day workers had their early breakfast and departed, taking each her neat lunch-pail,—they ate nothing of their employers;—and both kitchen and dining room would have stood idle till supper time. But the young manager knew she must work her plant for all it was worth, and speedily opened the dining room with the side entrance as a "Caffeteria," with the larger one as a sort of meeting place; papers and magazines on the tables.

From the counter you took what you liked, and seated yourself, and your friends, at one of the many small tables or in the flat-armed chairs in the big room, or on the broad piazza; and as this gave good food, cheapness, a chance for a comfortable seat and talk and a smoke, if one had time, it was largely patronized.

Mr. Thaddler, as an experienced *bon vivant,* despised sandwiches. "Picnicky makeshifts" he called them,—"railroad rations"—"bread and leavings," and when he saw these piles on piles of sandwiches, listed only as "No. 1," "No. 2" "No. 3," and so on, his benevolent intention wavered. But he pulled himself together and took a plateful, assorted.

"Come on, Porne," he said, "we'll play it's a Sunday school picnic," and he drew himself a cup of coffee, finding hot milk, cream and sugar crystals at hand. "I never saw a cheap joint where you could fix it yourself, before," he said,—and suspiciously tasted the mixture.

"By jing! That's coffee!" he cried in surprise. "There's no scum on the milk, and the cream's cream! Five cents! She won't get rich on this."

Then he applied himself to his "No. 1" sandwich, and his determined expression gave way to one of pleasure. "Why that's bread—real bread! I believe she made it herself!"

She did in truth,—she and Julianna with Hector as general assistant. The big oven was filled several times every morning: the fresh rolls disappeared at breakfast and supper, the fresh bread was packed in the lunch pails, and the stale bread was even now melting away in large bites behind the smiling mouths and mustaches of many men. Perfect bread, excellent butter, and "What's the filling I'd like to know?" More than one inquiring-minded patron split his sandwich to add sight to taste, but few could be sure of the flavorsome contents, fatless, gritless, smooth and even, covering the entire surface, the last mouthful as perfect as the first. Some were familiar, some new, all were delicious.

The six sandwiches were five cents, the cup of coffee five, and the little "drop cakes," sweet and spicy, were two for five. Every man spent fifteen cents, some of them more; and many took away small cakes in paper bags, if there were any left.

"I don't see how you can do it, and make a profit," urged Mr. Eltwood, making a pastorial call. "They are so good you know!"

Diantha smiled cheerfully. "That's because all your ideas are based on what we call 'domestic economy,' which is domestic waste. I buy in large quantities at wholesale rates, and my cook with her little helper, the two maids, and my own share of the work, of course, provides for the lot. Of course one has to know how."

"Whenever did you find—or did you create?—those heavenly sandwiches?" he asked.

"I have to thank my laundress for part of that success," she said. "She's a Dane, and it appears that the Danes are so fond of sandwiches that, in large establishments, they have a 'sandwich kitchen' to prepare them. It is quite a bit of work, but they are good and inexpensive. There is no limit to the variety."

As a matter of fact this lunch business paid well, and led to larger things.

The girl's methods were simple and so organized as to make one hand wash the other. Her house had some twenty-odd bedrooms, full accommodations for kitchen and laundry work on a large scale, big dining, dancing, and reception rooms, and broad shady piazzas on the sides. Its position on a corner near the business part of the little city, and at the foot of the hill crowned with so many millionaires and near millionaires as could get land there, offered many advantages, and every one was taken.

The main part of the undertaking was a House Worker's Union; a group of thirty girls, picked and trained. These, previously working out as servants, had received six dollars a week "and found." They now worked an agreed number of hours, were paid on a basis by the hour or day, and "found" themselves. Each had her own room, and the broad porches and ball room were theirs, except when engaged for dances and meetings of one sort and another.

It was a stirring year's work, hard but exciting, and the only difficulty which really worried Diantha was the same that worried the average housewife—the accounts.

CHAPTER XI: THE POWER OF THE SCREW

Your car is too big for one person to stir—
Your chauffeur is a little man, too;
Yet he lifts that machine, does the little chauffeur,
By the power of a gentle jackscrew.

Diantha worked.

For all her employees she demanded a ten-hour day, she worked fourteen; rising at six and not getting to bed till eleven, when her charges were all safely in their rooms for the night.

They were all up at five-thirty or thereabouts, breakfasting at six, and the girls off in time to reach their various places by seven. Their day was from 7 A. M. to 8.30 P. M., with half an hour out, from 11.30 to twelve, for their lunch; and three hours, between 2.20 and 5.30, for their own time, including their tea. Then they worked again from 5.30 to 8.30, on the dinner and the dishes, and then they came home to a pleasant nine o'clock supper, and had all hour to dance or rest before the 10.30 bell for bed time.

Special friends and "cousins" often came home with them, and frequently shared the supper—for a quarter—and the dance for nothing.

It was no light matter in the first place to keep twenty girls contented with such a regime, and working with the steady excellence required, and in the second place to keep twenty employers contented with them. There were failures on both sides; half a dozen families gave up the plan, and it took time to replace them; and three girls had to be asked to resign before the year was over. But most of them had been in training in the summer, and had listened for months to Diantha's earnest talks to the clubs, with good results.

"Remember we are not doing this for ourselves alone," she would say to them. "Our experiment is going to make this kind of work easier for all home workers everywhere. You may not like it at first, but neither did you like the old way. It will grow easier as we get used to it; and we *must* keep the rules, because we made them!"

She laboriously composed a neat little circular, distributed it widely, and kept a pile in her lunch room for people to take.

It read thus:

UNION HOUSE
Food and Service.

General Housework by the week $10.00
General Housework by the day $2.00
  Ten hours work a day, and furnish their own food.
Additional labor by the hour . . . .$.20
Special service for entertainments, maids and waitresses,
        by the hour . . . .$.25
  Catering for entertainments.
  Delicacies for invalids.
  Lunches packed and delivered.
Cafeteria. . . . . .12 to 2

What annoyed the young manager most was the uncertainty and irregularity involved in her work, the facts varying considerably from her calculations.

In the house all ran smoothly. Solemn Mrs. Thorvald did the laundry work for thirty-five—by the aid of her husband and a big mangle for the "flat work." The girls' washing was limited. "You have to be reasonable about it," Diantha had explained to them. "Your fifty cents covers a dozen pieces—no more. If you want more you have to pay more, just as your employers do for your extra time."

This last often happened. No one on the face of it could ask more than ten hours of the swift, steady work given by the girls at but a fraction over 14 cents an hour. Yet many times the housekeeper was anxious for more labor on special days; and the girls, unaccustomed to the three free hours in the afternoon, were quite willing to furnish it, thus adding somewhat to their cash returns.

They had a dressmaking class at the club afternoons, and as Union House boasted a good sewing machine, many of them spent the free hours in enlarging their wardrobes. Some amused themselves with light reading, a few studied, others met and walked outside. The sense of honest leisure grew upon them, with its broadening influence; and among her thirty Diantha found four or five who were able and ambitious, and willing to work heartily for the further development of the business.

Her two housemaids were specially selected. When the girls were out of the house these two maids washed the breakfast dishes with marvelous speed, and then helped Diantha prepare for the lunch. This was a large undertaking, and all three of them, as well as Julianna and Hector worked at it until some six or eight hundred sandwiches were ready, and two or three hundred little cakes.

Diantha had her own lunch, and then sat at the receipt of custom during the lunch hour, making change and ordering fresh supplies as fast as needed.

The two housemaids had a long day, but so arranged that it made but ten hours work, and they had much available time of their own. They had to be at work at 5:30 to set the table for six o'clock breakfast, and then they were at it steadily, with the dining rooms to "do," and the lunch to get ready, until 11:30, when they had an hour to eat and rest. From 12:30 to 4 o'clock they were busy with the lunch cups, the bed-rooms, and setting the table for dinner; but after that they had four hours to themselves, until the nine o'clock supper was over, and once more they washed dishes for half an hour. The caffeteria used only cups and spoons; the sandwiches and cakes were served on paper plates.

In the hand-cart methods of small housekeeping it is impossible to exact the swift precision of such work, but not in the standardized tasks and regular hours of such an establishment as this.

Diantha religiously kept her hour at noon, and tried to keep the three in the afternoon; but the employer and manager cannot take irresponsible rest as can the employee. She felt like a most inexperienced captain on a totally new species of ship, and her paper plans looked very weak sometimes, as bills turned out to be larger than she had allowed for, or her patronage unaccountably dwindled. But if the difficulties were great, the girl's courage was greater. "It is simply a big piece of work," she assured herself, "and may be a long one, but there never was anything better worth doing. Every new business has difficulties, I mustn't think of them. I must just push and push and push—a little more every day."

And then she would draw on all her powers to reason with, laugh at, and persuade some dissatisfied girl; or, hardest of all, to bring in a new one to fill a vacancy.

She enjoyed the details of her lunch business, and studied it carefully; planning for a restaurant a little later. Her bread was baked in long cylindrical closed pans, and cut by machinery into thin even slices, not a crust wasted; for they were ground into crumbs and used in the cooking.

The filling for her sandwiches was made from fish, flesh, and fowl; from cheese and jelly and fruit and vegetables; and so named or numbered that the general favorites were gradually determined.

Mr. Thaddler chatted with her over the counter, as far as she would allow it, and discoursed more fully with his friends on the verandah.

"Porne," he said, "where'd that girl come from anyway? She's a genius, that's what she is; a regular genius."

"She's all that," said Mr. Porne, "and a benefactor to humanity thrown in. I wish she'd start her food delivery, though. I'm tired of those two Swedes already. O—come from? Up in Jopalez, Inca County, I believe."

"New England stock I bet," said Mr. Thaddler. "Its a damn shame the way the women go on about her."

"Not all of them, surely," protested Mr. Porne.

"No, not all of 'em,—but enough of 'em to make mischief, you may be sure. Women are the devil, sometimes."

Mr. Porne smiled without answer, and Mr. Thaddler went sulking away—a bag of cakes bulging in his pocket.

The little wooden hotel in Jopalez boasted an extra visitor a few days later. A big red faced man, who strolled about among the tradesmen, tried the barber's shop, loafed in the post office, hired a rig and traversed the length and breadth of the town, and who called on Mrs. Warden, talking real estate with her most politely in spite of her protestation and the scornful looks of the four daughters; who bought tobacco and matches in the grocery store, and sat on the piazza thereof to smoke, as did other gentlemen of leisure.

Ross Warden occasionally leaned at the door jamb, with folded arms. He never could learn to be easily sociable with ranchmen and teamsters. Serve them he must, but chat with them he need not. The stout gentleman essayed some conversation, but did not get far. Ross was polite, but far from encouraging, and presently went home to supper, leaving a carrot-haired boy to wait upon his lingering customers.

"Nice young feller enough," said the stout gentleman to himself, "but raised on ramrods. Never got 'em from those women folks of his, either. He *has* a row to hoe!" And he departed as he had come.

Mr. Eltwood turned out an unexpectedly useful friend to Diantha. He steered club meetings and "sociables" into her large rooms, and as people found how cheap and easy it was to give parties that way, they continued the habit. He brought his doctor friends to sample the lunch, and they tested the value of Diantha's invalid cookery, and were more than pleased.

Hungry tourists were wholly without prejudice, and prized her lunches for their own sake. They descended upon the cafeteria in chattering swarms, some days, robbing the regular patrons of their food, and sent sudden orders for picnic lunches that broke in upon the routine hours of the place unmercifully.

But of all her patrons, the families of invalids appreciated Diantha's work the most. Where a little shack or tent was all they could afford to live in, or where the tiny cottage was more than filled with the patient, attending relative, and nurse, this depot of supplies was a relief indeed.

A girl could be had for an hour or two; or two girls, together, with amazing speed, could put a small house in dainty order while the sick man lay in his hammock under the pepper trees; and be gone before he was fretting for his bed again. They lived upon her lunches; and from them, and other quarters, rose an increasing demand for regular cooked food.

"Why don't you go into it at once?" urged Mrs. Weatherstone.

"I want to establish the day service first," said Diantha. "It is a pretty big business I find, and I do get tired sometimes. I can't afford to slip up, you know. I mean to take it up next fall, though."

"All right. And look here; see that you begin in first rate shape. I've got some ideas of my own about those food containers."

They discussed the matter more than once, Diantha most reluctant to take any assistance; Mrs. Weatherstone determined that she should.

"I feel like a big investor already," she said. "I don't think even you realize the *money* there is in this thing! You are interested in establishing the working girls, and saving money and time for the housewives. I am interested in making money out of it—honestly! It would be such a triumph!"

"You're very good—" Diantha hesitated.

"I'm not good. I'm most eagerly and selfishly interested. I've taken a new lease of life since knowing you, Diantha Bell! You see my father was a business man, and his father before him—I *like it*. There I was, with lots of money, and not an interest in life! Now?—why, there's no end to this thing, Diantha! It's one of the biggest businesses on earth—if not *the* biggest!"

"Yes—I know," the girl answered. "But its slow work. I feel the weight of it more than I expected. There's every reason to succeed, but there's the combined sentiment of the whole world to lift—it's as heavy as lead."

"Heavy! Of course it's heavy! The more fun to lift it! You'll do it, Diantha, I know you will, with that steady, relentless push of yours. But the cooked food is going to be your biggest power, and you must let me start it right. Now you listen to me, and make Mrs. Thaddler eat her words!"

Mrs. Thaddler's words would have proved rather poisonous, if eaten. She grew more antagonistic as the year advanced. Every fault that could be found in the undertaking she pounced upon and enlarged; every doubt that could be cast upon it she heavily piled up; and her opposition grew more rancorous as Mr. Thaddler enlarged in her hearing upon the excellence of Diantha's lunches and the wonders of her management.

"She's picked a bunch o' winners in those girls of hers," he declared to his friends. "They set out in the morning looking like a flock of sweet peas—in their pinks and whites and greens and vi'lets,—and do more work in an hour than the average slavey can do in three, I'm told."

It was a pretty sight to see those girls start out. They had a sort of uniform, as far as a neat gingham dress went, with elbow sleeves, white ruffled, and a Dutch collar; a sort of cross between a nurses dress and that of "La Chocolataire;" but colors were left to taste. Each carried her apron and a cap that covered the hair while cooking and sweeping; but nothing that suggested the black and white livery of the regulation servant.

"This is a new stage of labor," their leader reminded them. "You are not servants—you are employees. You wear a cap as an English carpenter does—or a French cook,—and an apron because your work needs it. It is not a ruffled label,—it's a business necessity. And each one of us must do our best to make this new kind of work valued and respected."

It is no easy matter to overcome prejudices many centuries old, and meet the criticism of women who have nothing to do but criticize. Those who were "mistresses," and wanted "servants,"—someone to do their will at any moment from early morning till late evening,—were not pleased with the new way if they tried it; but the women who had interests of their own to attend to; who merely wanted their homes kept clean, and the food well cooked and served, were pleased. The speed, the accuracy, the economy; the pleasant, quiet, assured manner of these skilled employees was a very different thing from the old slipshod methods of the ordinary general servant.

So the work slowly prospered, while Diantha began to put in execution the new plan she had been forced into.

While it matured, Mrs. Thaddler matured hers. With steady dropping she had let fall far and wide her suspicions as to the character of Union House.

"It looks pretty queer to me!" she would say, confidentially, "All those girls together, and no person to have any authority over them! Not a married woman in the house but that washerwoman,—and her husband's a fool!"

"And again; You don't see how she does it? Neither do I! The expenses must be tremendous—those girls pay next to nothing,—and all that broth and brown bread flying about town! Pretty queer doings, I think!"

"The men seem to like that caffeteria, don't they?" urged one caller, perhaps not unwilling to nestle Mrs. Thaddler, who flushed darkly as she replied. "Yes, they do. Men usually like that sort of place."

"They like good food at low prices, if that's what you mean," her visitor answered.

"That's not all I mean—by a long way," said Mrs. Thaddler. She said so much, and said it so ingeniously, that a dark rumor arose from nowhere, and grew rapidly. Several families discharged their Union House girls. Several girls complained that they were insultingly spoken to on the street. Even the lunch patronage began to fall off.

Diantha was puzzled—a little alarmed. Her slow, steady lifting of the prejudice against her was checked. She could not put her finger on the enemy, yet felt one distinctly, and had her own suspicions. But she also had her new move well arranged by this time.

Then a maliciously insinuating story of the place came out in a San Francisco paper, and a flock of local reporters buzzed in to sample the victim. They helped themselves to the luncheon, and liked it, but that did not soften their pens. They talked with such of the girls as they could get in touch with, and wrote such versions of these talks as suited them.

They called repeatedly at Union House, but Diantha refused to see them. Finally she was visited by the Episcopalian clergyman. He had heard her talk at the Club, was favorably impressed by the girl herself, and honestly distressed by the dark stories he now heard about Union House.

"My dear young lady," he said, "I have called to see you in your own interests. I do not, as you perhaps know, approve of your schemes. I consider them—ah—subversive of the best interests of the home! But I think you mean well, though mistakenly. Now I fear you are not aware that this-ah—ill-considered undertaking of yours, is giving rise to considerable adverse comment in the community. There is—ah—there is a great deal being said about this business of yours which I am sure you would regret if you knew it. Do you think it is wise; do you think it is—ah—right, my dear Miss Bell, to attempt to carry on a—a place of this sort, without the presence of a—of a Matron of assured standing?"

Diantha smiled rather coldly.

"May I trouble you to step into the back parlor, Dr.

Aberthwaite," she said; and then;

"May I have the pleasure of presenting to you Mrs. Henderson Bell—my mother?"

* * * *

"Wasn't it great!" said Mrs. Weatherstone; "I was there you see,—I'd come to call on Mrs. Bell—she's a dear,—and in came Mrs. Thaddler—"

"Mrs. Thaddler?"

"O I know it was old Aberthwaite, but he represented Mrs. Thaddler and her clique, and had come there to preach to Diantha about propriety—I heard him,—and she brought him in and very politely introduced him to her mother!—it was rich, Isabel."

"How did Diantha manage it?" asked her friend.

"She's been trying to arrange it for ever so long. Of course her father objected—you'd know that. But there's a sister—not a bad sort, only very limited; she's taken the old man to board, as it were, and I guess the mother really set her foot down for once—said she had a right to visit her own daughter!"

"It would seem so," Mrs. Porne agreed. "I *am* so glad! It will be so much easier for that brave little woman now."

It was.

Diantha held her mother in her arms the night she came, and cried tike a baby.

"O mother *dear!*" she sobbed, "I'd no idea I should miss you so much. O you blessed comfort!"

Her mother cried a bit too; she enjoyed this daughter more than either of her older children, and missed her more. A mother loves all her children, naturally; but a mother is also a person— and may, without sin, have personal preferences.

She took hold of Diantha's tangled mass of papers with the eagerness of a questing hound.

"You've got all the bills, of course," she demanded, with her anxious rising inflection.

"Every one," said the girl. "You taught me that much. What

puzzles me is to make things balance. I'm making more than I thought in some lines, and less in others, and I can't make it come out straight."

"It won't, altogether, till the end of the year I dare say," said Mrs. Bell, "but let's get clear as far as we can. In the first place we must separate your business,—see how much each one pays."

"The first one I want to establish," said her daughter, "is the girl's club. Not just this one, with me to run it. But to show that any group of twenty or thirty girls could do this thing in any city. Of course where rents and provisions were high they'd have to charge more. I want to make an average showing somehow. Now can you disentangle the girl part front the lunch part and the food part, mother dear, and make it all straight?"

Mrs. Bell could and did; it gave her absolute delight to do it. She set down the total of Diantha's expenses so far in the Service Department, as follows:

Rent of Union House	$1,500
Rent of furniture	$300
One payment on furniture	$400
Fuel and lights, etc	$352
Service of 5 at $10 a week each	$2,600
Food for thirty-seven	$3,848
Total	$9,000

"That covers everything but my board," said Mrs. Bell.

"Now your income is easy—35 x $4.50 equals $8,190. Take that from your $9,000 and you are $810 behind."

"Yes, I know," said Diantha, eagerly, "but if it was merely a girl's club home, the rent and fixtures would be much less. A home could be built, with thirty bedrooms—and all necessary conveniences—for $7,000. I've asked Mr. and Mrs. Porne about it; and the furnishing needn't cost over $2,000 if it was very plain. Ten per cent. of that is a rent of $900 you see."

"I see," said her mother. "Better say a thousand. I guess it could be done for that."

So they set down rent, $1,000.

"There have to be five paid helpers in the house," Diantha went on, "the cook, the laundress, the two maids, and the matron. She must buy and manage. She could be one of their mothers or aunts."

Mrs. Bell smiled. "Do you really imagine, Diantha, that Mrs. O'Shaughnessy or Mrs. Yon Yonson can manage a house like this as you can?"

Diantha flushed a little. "No, mother, of course not. But I am keeping very full reports of all the work. Just the schedule of labor—the hours—the exact things done. One laundress, with machinery, can wash for thirty-five, (its only six a day you see), and the amount is regulated; about six dozen a day, and all the flat work mangled.

"In a Girl's Club alone the cook has all day off, as it were; she can do the down stairs cleaning. And the two maids have only table service and bedrooms."

"Thirty-five bedrooms?"

"Yes. But two girls together, who know how, can do a room in 8 minutes—easily. They are small and simple you see. Make the bed, shake the mats, wipe the floors and windows,—you watch them!"

"I have watched them," the mother admitted. "They are as quick as—as mill-workers!"

"Well," pursued Diantha, "they spend three hours on dishes and tables, and seven on cleaning. The bedrooms take 280 minutes; that's nearly five hours. The other two are for the bath rooms, halls, stairs, downstairs windows, and so on. That's all right. Then I'm keeping the menus—just what I furnish and what it costs. Anybody could order and manage when it was all set down for her. And you see—as you have figured it— they'd have over $500 leeway to buy the furniture if they were allowed to."

"Yes," Mrs. Bell admitted, "*if* the rent was what you allow, and *if* they all work all the time!"

"That's the hitch, of course. But mother; the girls who don't have steady jobs do work by the hour, and that brings in more, on the whole. If they are the right kind they can make good. If they find anyone who don't keep her job—for good reasons— they can drop her."

"M'm!" said Mrs. Bell. "Well, it's an interesting experiment. But how about you? So far you are $410 behind."

"Yes, because my rent's so big. But I cover that by letting the rooms, you see."

Mrs. Bell considered the orders of this sort. "So far it averages about $25.00 a week; that's doing well."

"It will be less in summer—much less," Diantha suggested. "Suppose you call it an average of $15.00."

"Call it $10.00," said her mother ruthlessly. "At that it covers your deficit and $110 over."

"Which isn't much to live on," Diantha agreed, "but then comes my special catering, and the lunches."

Here they were quite at sea for a while. But as the months passed, and the work steadily grew on their hands, Mrs. Bell became more and more cheerful. She was up with the earliest, took entire charge of the financial part of the concern, and at last Diantha was able to rest fully in her afternoon hours. What delighted her most was to see her mother thrive in the work. Her thin shoulders lifted a little as small dragging tasks were forgotten and a large growing business substituted. Her eyes grew bright again, she held her head as she did in her keen girlhood, and her daughter felt fresh hope and power as she saw already the benefit of the new method as affecting her nearest and dearest.

All Diantha's friends watched the spread of the work with keenly sympathetic intent; but to Mrs. Weatherstone it became almost as fascinating as to the girl herself.

"It's going to be one of the finest businesses in the world!" she said, "And one of the largest and best paying. Now I'll have a surprise ready for that girl in the spring, and another next year, if I'm not mistaken!"

There were long and vivid discussions of the matter between her and her friends the Pornes, and Mrs. Porne spent more hours in her "drawing room" than she had for years.

But while these unmentioned surprises were pending, Mrs. Weatherstone departed to New York—to Europe; and was gone some months. In the spring she returned, in April—which is late June in Orchardina. She called upon Diantha and her mother at once, and opened her attack.

"I do hope, Mrs. Bell, that you'll back me up," she said. "You have the better business head I think, in the financial line."

"She has," Diantha admitted. "She's ten times as good as I am at that; but she's no more willing to carry obligation than I am, Mrs. Weatherstone."

"Obligation is one thing—investment is another," said her guest. "I live on my money—that is, on other people's work. I am a base capitalist, and you seem to me good material to invest in. So—take it or leave it—I've brought you an offer."

She then produced from her hand bag some papers, and, from her car outside, a large object carefully boxed, about the size and shape of a plate warmer. This being placed on the table before them, was uncovered, and proved to be a food container of a new model.

"I had one made in Paris," she explained, "and the rest copied here to save paying duty. Lift it!"

They lifted it in amazement—it was so light.

"Aluminum," she said, proudly, "Silver plated—new process! And bamboo at the corners you see. All lined and interlined with asbestos, rubber fittings for silver ware, plate racks, food compartments—see?"

She pulled out drawers, opened little doors, and rapidly laid out a table service for five.

"It will hold food for five—the average family, you know. For larger orders you'll have to send more. I had to make *some* estimate."

"What lovely dishes!" said Diantha.

"Aren't they! Aluminum, silvered! If your washers are careful they won't get dented, and you can't break 'em."

Mrs. Bell examined the case and all its fittings with eager attention.

"It's the prettiest thing I ever saw," she said. "Look, Diantha; here's for soup, here's for water—or wine if you want, all your knives and forks at the side, Japanese napkins up here. Its lovely, but—I should think—expensive!"

Mrs. Weatherstone smiled. "I've had twenty-five of them made. They cost, with the fittings, $100 apiece, $2,500. I will rent them to you, Miss Bell, at a rate of 10 per cent. interest; only $250 a year!"

"It ought to take more," said Mrs. Bell, "there'll be breakage and waste."

"You can't break them, I tell you," said the cheerful visitor, "and dents can be smoothed out in any tin shop—you'll have to pay for it;—will that satisfy you?"

Diantha was looking at her, her eyes deep with gratitude. "I—you know what I think of you!" she said.

Mrs. Weatherstone laughed. "I'm not through yet," she said. "Look at my next piece of impudence!" This was only on paper, but the pictures were amply illuminating.

"I went to several factories," she gleefully explained, "here and abroad. A Yankee firm built it. It's in my garage now!"

It was a light gasolene motor wagon, the body built like those old-fashioned moving wagons which were also used for excursions, wherein the floor of the vehicle was rather narrow, and set low, and the seats ran lengthwise, widening out over the wheels; only here the wheels were lower, and in the space under the seats ran a row of lockers opening outside. Mrs. Weatherstone smiled triumphantly.

"Now, Diantha Bell," she said, "here's something you haven't thought of, I do believe! This estimable vehicle will carry thirty people inside easily," and she showed them how each side held twelve, and turn-up seats accommodated six more;

"and outside,"—she showed the lengthwise picture—"it carries twenty-four containers. If you want to send all your twenty-five at once, one can go here by the driver.

"Now then. This is not an obligation, Miss Bell, it is another valuable investment. I'm having more made. I expect to have use for them in a good many places. This cost pretty near $3,000, and you get it at the same good interest, for $300 a year. What's more, if you are smart enough—and I don't doubt you are,—you can buy the whole thing on installments, same as you mean to with your furniture."

Diantha was dumb, but her mother wasn't. She thanked Mrs. Weatherstone with a hearty appreciation of her opportune help, but no less of her excellent investment.

"Don't be a goose, Diantha," she said. "You will set up your food business in first class style, and I think you can carry it successfully. But Mrs. Weatherstone's right; she's got a new investment here that'll pay her better than most others—and be a growing thing I do believe."

And still Diantha found it difficult to express her feelings. She had lived under a good deal of strain for many months now, and this sudden opening out of her plans was a heavenly help indeed.

Mrs. Weatherstone went around the table and sat by her. "Child," said she, "you don't begin to realize what you've done for me—and for Isobel—and for ever so many in this town, and all over the world. And besides, don't you think anybody else can see your dream? We can't *do* it as you can, but we can see what it's going to mean,—and we'll help if we can. You wouldn't grudge us that, would you?"

As a result of all this the cooked food delivery service was opened at once.

"It is true that the tourists are gone, mostly," said Mrs. Weatherstone, as she urged it, "but you see there are ever so many residents who have more trouble with servants in summer than they do in winter, and hate to have a fire in the house, too."

So Diantha's circulars had an addition, forthwith.

These were distributed among the Orchardinians, setting their tongues wagging anew, as a fresh breeze stirs the eaves of the forest.

The stealthy inroads of lunches and evening refreshments had been deprecated already; this new kind of servant who wasn't a servant, but held her head up like anyone else ("They are as independent as—as—'salesladies,'" said one critic), was also viewed with alarm; but when even this domestic assistant was to be removed, and a square case of food and dishes substituted, all Archaic Orchardina was horrified.

There were plenty of new minds in the place, however; enough to start Diantha with seven full orders and five partial ones.

Her work at the club was now much easier, thanks to her mother's assistance, to the smoother running of all the machinery with the passing of time, and further to the fact that most of her girls were now working at summer resorts, for shorter hours and higher wages. They paid for their rooms at the club still, but the work of the house was so much lightened that each of the employees was given two weeks of vacation— on full pay.

The lunch department kept on a pretty regular basis from the patronage of resident business men, and the young manager—in her ambitious moments—planned for enlarging it in the winter. But during the summer her whole energies went to perfecting the *menus* and the service of her food delivery.

Mrs. Porne was the very first to order. She had been waiting impatiently for a chance to try the plan, and, with her husband, had the firmest faith in Diantha's capacity to carry it through.

"We don't save much in money," she explained to the eager Mrs. Ree, who hovered, fascinated, over the dangerous topic, "but we do in comfort, I can tell you. You see I had two girls, paid them $12 a week; now I keep just the one, for $6. My food and fuel for the four of us (I don't count the babies either time— they remain as before), was all of $16, often more. That made

$28 a week. Now I pay for three meals a day, delivered, for three of us, $15 a week—with the nurse's wages, $21. Then I pay a laundress one day, $2, and her two meals, $.50, making $23.50. Then I have two maids, for an hour a day, to clean; $.50 a day for six days, $3, and one maid Sunday, $.25. $26.75 in all. So we only make $1.25. *But!* there's another room! We have the cook's room for an extra guest; I use it most for a sewing room, though and the kitchen is a sort of day nursery now. The house seems as big again!"

"But the food?" eagerly inquired Mrs. Ree. "Is it as good as your own? Is it hot and tempting?"

Mrs. Ree was fascinated by the new heresy. As a staunch adherent of the old Home and Culture Club, and its older ideals, she disapproved of the undertaking, but her curiosity was keen about it.

Mrs. Porne smiled patiently. "You remember Diantha Bell's cooking I am sure, Mrs. Ree," she said. "And Julianna used to cook for dinner parties—when one could get her. My Swede was a very ordinary cook, as most of these untrained girls are. Do take off your hat and have dinner with us,—I'll show you," urged Mrs. Porne.

"I—O I mustn't," fluttered the little woman. "They'll expect me at home—and—surely your—supply—doesn't allow for guests?"

"We'll arrange all that by 'phone," her hostess explained; and she promptly sent word to the Ree household, then called up Union House and ordered one extra dinner.

"Is it—I'm dreadfully rude I know, but I'm *so* interested! Is it—expensive?"

Mrs. Porne smiled. "Haven't you seen the little circular? Here's one, 'Extra meals to regular patrons 25 cents.' And no more trouble to order than to tell a maid."

Mrs. Ree had a lively sense of paltering with Satan as she sat down to the Porne's dinner table. She had seen the delivery wagon drive to the door, had heard the man deposit something heavy on the back porch, and was now confronted by a butler's tray at Mrs. Porne's left, whereon stood a neat square shining object with silvery panels and bamboo trimmings.

"It's not at all bad looking, is it?" she ventured.

"Not bad enough to spoil one's appetite," Mr. Porne cheerily agreed.

"Open, Sesame! Now you know the worst."

Mrs. Porne opened it, and an inner front was shown, with various small doors and drawers.

"Do you know what is in it?" asked the guest.

"No, thank goodness, I don't," replied her hostess. "If there's anything tiresome it is to order meals and always know what's coming! That's what men get so tired of at restaurants; what they hate so when their wives ask them what they want for dinner. Now I can enjoy my dinner at my own table, just as if I was a guest."

"It is—a tax—sometimes," Mrs. Ree admitted, adding hastily, "But one is glad to do it—to make home attractive."

Mr. Porne's eyes sought his wife's, and love and contentment flashed between them, as she quietly set upon the table three silvery plates.

"Not silver, surely!" said Mrs. Ree, lifting hers, "Oh, aluminum."

"Aluminum, silver plated," said Mr. Porne. "They've learned how to do it at last. It's a problem of weight, you see, and breakage. Aluminum isn't pretty, glass and silver are heavy, but we all love silver, and there's a pleasant sense of gorgeousness in this outfit."

It did look rather impressive; silver tumblers, silver dishes, the whole dainty service—and so surprisingly light.

"You see she knows that it is very important to please the eye as well as the palate," said Mr. Porne. "Now speaking of palates, let us all keep silent and taste this soup." They did keep silent in supreme contentment while the soup lasted. Mrs. Ree laid down her spoon with the air of one roused from a lovely dream.

"Why—why—it's like Paris," she said in an awed tone.

"Isn't it?" Mr. Porne agreed, "and not twice alike in a month,

I think."

"Why, there aren't thirty kinds of soup, are there?" she urged.

"I never thought there were when we kept servants," said he. "Three was about their limit, and greasy, at that."

Mrs. Porne slipped the soup plates back in their place and served the meat.

"She does not give a fish course, does she?" Mrs. Ree observed.

"Not at the table d'hote price," Mrs. Porne answered. "We never pretended to have a fish course ourselves—do you?" Mrs. Ree did not, and eagerly disclaimed any desire for fish. The meat was roast beef, thinly sliced, hot and juicy.

"Don't you miss the carving, Mr. Porne?" asked the visitor. "I do so love to see a man at the head of his own table, carving."

"I do miss it, Mrs. Ree. I miss it every day of my life with devout thankfulness. I never was a good carver, so it was no pleasure to me to show off; and to tell you the truth, when I come to the table, I like to eat—not saw wood." And Mr. Porne ate with every appearance of satisfaction.

"We never get roast beef like this I'm sure," Mrs. Ree admitted, "we can't get it small enough for our family."

"And a little roast is always spoiled in the cooking. Yes this is far better than we used to have," agreed her hostess.

Mrs. Ree enjoyed every mouthful of her meal. The soup was hot. The salad was crisp and the ice cream hard. There was sponge cake, thick, light, with sugar freckles on the dark crust. The coffee was perfect and almost burned the tongue.

"I don't understand about the heat and cold," she said; and they showed her the asbestos-lined compartments and perfectly fitting places for each dish and plate. Everything went back out of sight; small leavings in a special drawer, knives and forks held firmly by rubber fittings, nothing that shook or rattled. And the case was set back by the door where the man called for it at eight o'clock.

"She doesn't furnish table linen?"

"No, there are Japanese napkins at the top here. We like our own napkins, and we didn't use a cloth, anyway."

"And how about silver?"

"We put ours away. This plated ware they furnish is perfectly good. We could use ours of course if we wanted to wash it. Some do that and some have their own case marked, and their own silver in it, but it's a good deal of risk, I think, though they are extremely careful."

Mrs. Ree experienced peculiarly mixed feelings. As far as food went, she had never eaten a better dinner. But her sense of Domestic Aesthetics was jarred.

"It certainly tastes good," she said. "Delicious, in fact. I am extremely obliged to you, Mrs. Porne, I'd no idea it could be sent so far and be so good. And only five dollars a week, you say?"

"For each person, yes."

"I don't see how she does it. All those cases and dishes, and the delivery wagon!"

That was the universal comment in Orchardina circles as the months passed and Union House continued in existence— "I don't see how she does it!"

CHAPTER XII: LIKE A BANYAN TREE

The Earth-Plants spring up from beneath,
The Air-Plants swing down from above,
But the Banyan trees grow
Both above and below,
And one makes a prosperous grove.

In the fleeting opportunities offered by the Caffeteria, and in longer moments, rather neatly planned for, with some remnants of an earlier ingenuity, Mr. Thaddler contrived to become acquainted with Mrs. Bell. Diantha never quite liked him, but he won her mother's heart by frank praise of the girl and her ventures.

"I never saw a smarter woman in my life," he said; "and no airs. I tell you, ma'am, if there was more like her this world would be an easier place to live in, and I can see she owes it all to you, ma'am."

This the mother would never admit for a moment, but expatiated loyally on the scientific mind of Mr. Henderson Bell, still of Jopalez.

"I don't see how he can bear to let her out of his sight," said Mr. Thaddler.

"Of course he hated to let her go," replied the lady. "We both did. But he is very proud of her now."

"I guess there's somebody else who's proud of her, too," he suggested. "Excuse me, ma'am, I don't mean to intrude, but we know there must be a good reason for your daughter keeping all Orchardina at a distance. Why, she could have married six times over in her first year here!"

"She does not wish to give up her work," Mrs. Bell explained.

"Of course not; and why should she? Nice, womanly business, I am sure. I hope nobody'd expect a girl who can keep house for a whole township to settle down to bossing one man and a hired girl."

In course of time he got a pretty clear notion of how matters stood, and meditated upon it, seriously rolling his big cigar about between pursed lips. Mr. Thaddler was a good deal of a gossip, but this he kept to himself, and did what he could to enlarge the patronage of Union House.

The business grew. It held its own in spite of fluctuations, and after a certain point began to spread steadily. Mrs. Bell's coming and Mr. Eltwood's ardent championship, together with Mr. Thaddler's, quieted the dangerous slanders which had imperilled the place at one time. They lingered, subterraneously, of course. People never forget slanders. A score of years after there were to be found in Orchardina folk who still whispered about dark allegations concerning Union House; and the papers had done some pretty serious damage; but the fame of good food, good service, cheapness and efficiency made steady headway.

In view of the increase and of the plans still working in her mind, Diantha made certain propositions to Mr. Porne, and also to Mrs. Porne, in regard to a new, specially built club-house for the girls.

"I have proved what they can do, with me to manage them, and want now to prove that they can do it themselves, with any matron competent to follow my directions. The house need not be so expensive; one big dining-room, with turn-up tables like those ironing-board seat-tables, you know—then they can dance there. Small reception room and office, hall, kitchen and laundry, and thirty bedrooms, forty by thirty, with an "ell" for the laundry, ought to do it, oughtn't it?"

Mrs. Porne agreed to make plans, and did so most successfully, and Mr. Porne found small difficulty in persuading an investor to put up such a house, which visibly could be used as a boarding-house or small hotel, if it failed in its first purpose.

It was built of concrete, a plain simple structure, but fine in proportions and pleasantly colored.

Diantha kept her plans to herself, as usual, but they grew so fast that she felt a species of terror sometimes, lest the ice break somewhere.

"Steady, now!" she would say. "This is real business, just plain business. There's no reason why I shouldn't succeed as well as Fred Harvey. I will succeed. I am succeeding."

She kept well, she worked hard, she was more than glad to have her mother with her; but she wanted something else, which seemed farther off than ever. Her lover's picture hung on the wall of her bedroom, stood on her bureau, and (but this was a secret) a small one was carried in her bosom.

Rather a grim looking young woman, Diantha, with the cares of the world of house-keepers upon her proud young shoulders; with all the stirring hopes to be kept within bounds, all the skulking fears to be resisted, and the growing burden of a large affair to be carried steadily.

But when she woke, in the brilliant California mornings, she would lie still a few moments looking at the face on the wall and the face on the bureau; would draw the little picture out from under her pillow and kiss it, would say to herself for the thousandth time, "It is for him, too."

She missed him, always.

The very vigor of her general attitude, the continued strength with which she met the days and carried them, made it all the more needful for her to have some one with whom she could forget every care, every purpose, every effort; some one who would put strong arms around her and call her "Little Girl." His letters were both a comfort and a pain. He was loyal, kind, loving, but always that wall of disapproval. He loved her, he did not love her work.

She read them over and over, hunting anew for the tender phrases, the things which seemed most to feed and comfort her. She suffered not only from her loneliness, but from his; and most keenly from his sternly suppressed longing for freedom and the work that belonged to him.

"Why can't he see," she would say to herself, "that if this succeeds, he can do his work; that I can make it possible for him? And he won't let me. He won't take it from me. Why are men so proud? Is there anything so ignominious about a woman that it is disgraceful to let one help you? And why can't he think at all about the others? It's not just us, it's all people. If this works, men will have easier times, as well as women. Everybody can do their real work better with this old primitive business once set right."

And then it was always time to get up, or time to go to bed, or time to attend to some of the numberless details of her affairs.

She and her mother had an early lunch before the cafeteria opened, and were glad of the afternoon tea, often held in a retired corner of the broad piazza. She sat there one hot, dusty afternoon, alone and unusually tired. The asphalted street was glaring and noisy, the cross street deep in soft dust, for months unwet.

Failure had not discouraged her, but increasing success with all its stimulus and satisfaction called for more and more power. Her mind was busy foreseeing, arranging, providing for emergencies; and then the whole thing slipped away from her, she dropped her head upon her arm for a moment, on the edge of the tea table, and wished for Ross.

From down the street and up the street at this moment, two men were coming; both young, both tall, both good looking, both apparently approaching Union House. One of them was the nearer, and his foot soon sounded on the wooden step. The other stopped and looked in a shop window.

Diantha started up, came forward,—it was Mr. Eltwood. She had a vague sense of disappointment, but received him cordially. He stood there, his hat off, holding her hand for a long moment, and gazing at her with evident admiration. They turned and sat down in the shadow of the reed-curtained corner.

The man at the shop window turned, too, and went away.

Mr. Eltwood had been a warm friend and cordial supporter from the epoch of the Club-splitting speech. He had helped materially in the slow, up-hill days of the girl's effort, with faith and kind words. He had met the mother's coming with most friendly advances, and Mrs. Bell found herself much at home in his liberal little church.

Diantha had grown to like and trust him much.

"What's this about the new house, Miss Bell? Your mother says I may know."

"Why not?" she said. "You have followed this thing from the first. Sugar or lemon? You see I want to disentangle the undertakings, set them upon their own separate feet, and establish the practical working of each one."

"I see," he said, "and 'day service' is not 'cooked food delivery.'"

"Nor yet 'rooms for entertainment'," she agreed. "We've got them all labelled, mother and I. There's the 'd. s.' and 'c. f. d.' and 'r. f. e.' and the 'p. p.' That's picnics and parties. And more coming."

"What, more yet? You'll kill yourself, Miss Bell. Don't go

too fast. You are doing a great work for humanity. Why not take a little more time?"

"I want to do it as quickly as I can, for reasons," answered Diantha.

Mr. Eltwood looked at her with tender understanding. "I don't want to intrude any further than you are willing to want me," he said, "but sometimes I think that even you—strong as you are—would be better for some help."

She did not contradict him. Her hands were in her lap, her eyes on the worn boards of the piazza floor. She did not see a man pass on the other side of the street, cast a searching glance across and walk quickly on again.

"If you were quite free to go on with your beautiful work," said Mr. Eltwood slowly, "if you were offered heartiest appreciation, profound respect, as well as love, of course; would you object to marrying, Miss Bell?" asked in an even voice, as if it were a matter of metaphysical inquiry. Mrs. Porne had told him of her theory as to a lover in the home town, wishing to save him a long heart ache, but he was not sure of it, and he wanted to be.

Diantha glanced quickly at him, and felt the emotion under his quiet words. She withdrew her eyes, looking quite the other way.

"You are enough of a friend to know, Mr. Eltwood," she said, "I rather thought you did know. I am engaged."

"Thank you for telling me; some one is greatly to be congratulated," he spoke sincerely, and talked quietly on about less personal matters, holding his tea untasted till it was cold.

"Do let me give you some that is hot," she said at last, "and let me thank you from my heart for the help and strength and comfort you have been to me, Mr. Eltwood."

"I'm very glad," he said; and again, "I am very glad." "You may count upon anything I can do for you, always," he continued. "I am proud to be your friend."

He held her hand once more for a moment, and went away with his head up and a firm step. To one who watched him go, he had almost a triumphant air, but it was not triumph, only the brave beginning of a hard fight and a long one.

Then came Mrs. Bell, returned from a shopping trip, and sank down in a wicker rocker, glad of the shade and a cup of tea. No, she didn't want it iced. "Hot tea makes you cooler," was her theory.

"You don't look very tired," said the girl. "Seems to me you get stronger all the time."

"I do," said her mother. "You don't realize, you can't realize, Diantha, what this means to me. Of course to you I am an old woman, a back number—one has to feel so about one's mother. I did when I married, and my mother then was five years younger than I am now."

"I don't think you old, mother, not a bit of it. You ought to have twenty or thirty years of life before you, real life."

"That's just what I'm feeling," said Mrs. Bell, "as if I'd just begun to live! This is so *different!* There is a big, moving thing to work for. There is—why Diantha, you wouldn't believe what a comfort it is to me to feel that my work here is—really— adding to the profits!"

Diantha laughed aloud.

"You dear old darling," she said, "I should think it was! It is *making* the profits."

"And it grows so," her mother went on. "Here's this part so well assured that you're setting up the new Union House! Are you *sure* about Mrs. Jessup, dear?"

"As sure as I can be of any one till I've tried a long time. She has done all I've asked her to here, and done it well. Besides, I mean to keep a hand on it for a year or two yet—I can't afford to have that fail."

Mrs. Jessup was an imported aunt, belonging to one of the cleverest girls, and Diantha had had her in training for some weeks.

"Well, I guess she's as good as any you'd be likely to get," Mrs. Bell admitted, "and we mustn't expect paragons. If this can't be done by an average bunch of working women the world over, it can't be done—that's all!"

"It can be done," said the girl, calmly. "It will be done. You see."

"Mr. Thaddler says you could run any kind of a business you set your hand to," her mother went on. "He has a profound respect for your abilities, Dina."

"Seems to me you and Mr. Thaddler have a good deal to say to each other, motherkins. I believe you enjoy that caffeteria desk, and all the compliments you get."

"I do," said Mrs. Bell stoutly. "I do indeed! Why, I haven't seen so many men, to speak to, since—why, never in my life! And they are very amusing—some of them. They like to come here—like it immensely. And I don't wonder. I believe you'll do well to enlarge."

Then they plunged into a discussion of the winter's plans. The day service department and its employment agency was to go on at the New Union House, with Mrs. Jessup as manager; the present establishment was to be run as a hotel and restaurant, and the depot for the cooked food delivery.

Mrs. Thorvald and her husband were installed by themselves in another new venture; a small laundry outside the town. This place employed several girls steadily, and the motor wagon found a new use between meals, in collecting and delivering laundry parcels.

"It simplifies it a lot—to get the washing out of the place and the girls off my mind," said Diantha. "Now I mean to buckle down and learn the hotel business—thoroughly, and develop this cooked food delivery to perfection."

"Modest young lady," smiled her mother. "Where do you mean to stop—if ever?"

"I don't mean to stop till I'm dead," Diantha answered; "but I don't mean to undertake any more trades, if that is what you mean. You know what I'm after—to get 'housework' on a business basis, that's all; and prove, prove, PROVE what a good business it is. There's the cleaning branch—that's all started and going well in the day service. There's the washing—that's simple and easy. Laundry work's no mystery. But the food part is a big thing. It's an art, a science, a business, and a handicraft. I had the handicraft to start with; I'm learning the business; but I've got a lot to learn yet in the science and art of it."

"Don't do too much at once," her mother urged. "You've got to cater to people as they are."

"I know it," the girl agreed. "They must be led, step by step—the natural method. It's a big job, but not too big. Out of all the women who have done housework for so many ages, surely it's not too much to expect one to have a special genius for it!"

Her mother gazed at her with loving admiration.

"That's just what you have, Dina—a special genius for house-work. I wish there were more of you!"

"There are plenty of me, mother dear, only they haven't come out. As soon as I show 'em how to make the thing pay, you'll find that we have a big percentage of this kind of ability. It's all buried now in the occasional 'perfect housekeeper.'"

"But they won't leave their husbands, Dina."

"They don't need to," the girl answered cheerfully. "Some of them aren't married yet; some of them have lost their husbands, and *some* of them"—she said this a little bitterly—"have husbands who will be willing to let their wives grow."

"Not many, I'm afraid," said Mrs. Bell, also with some gloom.

Diantha lightened up again. "Anyhow, here you are, mother dear! And for this year I propose that you assume the financial management of the whole business at a salary of $1,000 'and found.' How does that suit you?"

Mrs. Bell looked at her unbelievingly.

"You can't afford it, Dina!"

"Oh, yes, I can—you know I can, because you've got the accounts. I'm going to make big money this year."

"But you'll need it. This hotel and restaurant business may not do well."

"Now, mother, you *know* we're doing well. Look here!" And Diantha produced her note-book.

"Here's the little laundry place; its fittings come to so much, wages so much, collection and delivery so much, supplies so much—and already enough patronage engaged to cover. It will be bigger in winter, a lot, with transients, and this hotel to fall back on; ought to clear at least a thousand a year. The service club don't pay me anything, of course; that is for the girls' benefit; but the food delivery is doing better than I dared hope."

Mrs. Bell knew the figures better than Diantha, even, and they went over them carefully again. If the winter's patronage held on to equal the summer's—and the many transient residents ought to increase it—they would have an average of twenty families a week to provide for—one hundred persons.

The expenses were:

Food for 100 at $250 a week. Per capita. $600
                                                          ———
                                                   per year $13,000

Labor—delivery man. $600
Head cook. $600
Two assistant cooks.. . . . .$1,040
Three washers and packers. $1,560
Office girl. . . . .
                                                          ———
                                                   Per year $4,320

Rent, kitchen, office, etc. $500
Rent of motor.. . . . . $300
Rent of cases. $250
Gasolene and repairs. . . . .
                                                          ———
                                                   Per year $1,680

                                                   Total. $19,000

"How do you make the gasolene and repairs as much as that?" asked Mrs. Bell.

"It's margin, mother—makes it even money. It won't be so much, probably."

The income was simple and sufficient. They charged $5.00 a week per capita for three meals, table d'hote, delivered thrice daily. Frequent orders for extra meals really gave them more than they set down, but the hundred-person estimate amounted to $26,000 a year.

"Now, see," said Diantha triumphantly; "subtract all that expense list (and it is a liberal one), and we have $7,000 left. I can buy the car and the cases this year and have $1,600 over! More; because if I do buy them I can leave off some of the interest, and the rent of kitchen and office comes to Union House! Then there's all of the extra orders. It's going to pay splendidly, mother! It clears $70 a year per person. Next year it will clear a lot more."

It did not take long to make Mrs. Bell admit that if the business went on as it had been going Diantha would be able to pay her a salary of a thousand dollars, and have five hundred left— from the food business alone.

There remained the hotel, with large possibilities. The present simple furnishings were to be moved over to New Union House, and paid for by the girls in due time. With new paint, paper, and furniture, the old house would make a very comfortable place.

"Of course, it's the restaurant mainly—these big kitchens and the central location are the main thing. The guests will be mostly tourists, I suppose."

Diantha dwelt upon the prospect at some length; and even her cautious mother had to admit that unless there was some setback the year had a prospect of large success.

"How about all this new furnishing?" Mrs. Bell said suddenly. "How do you cover that? Take what you've got ahead now?"

"Yes; there's plenty," said Diantha. "You see, there is all Union House has made, and this summer's profit on the cooked food—it's plenty."

"Then you can't pay for the motor and cases as you planned," her mother insisted.

"No, not unless the hotel and restaurant pays enough to make good. But I don't *have* to buy them the first year. If I don't, there is $5,500 leeway."

"Yes, you are safe enough; there's over $4,000 in the bank now," Mrs. Bell admitted. "But, child," she said suddenly, "your father!"

"Yes, I've thought of father," said the girl, "and I mean to ask him to come and live at the hotel. I think he'd like it. He could meet people and talk about his ideas, and I'm sure I'd like to have him."

They talked much and long about this, till the evening settled about them, till they had their quiet supper, and the girls came home to their noisy one; and late that evening, when all was still again, Diantha came to the dim piazza corner once more and sat there quite alone.

Full of hope, full of courage, sure of her progress—and aching with loneliness.

She sat with her head in her hands, and to her ears came suddenly the sound of a familiar step—a well-known voice—the hands and the lips of her lover.

"Diantha!" He held her close.

"Oh, Ross! Ross! Darling! Is it true? When did you come? Oh, I'm so glad! So *glad* to see you!"

She was so glad that she had to cry a little on his shoulder, which he seemed to thoroughly enjoy.

"I've good news for you, little girl," he said. "Good news at last! Listen, dear; don't cry. There's an end in sight. A man has bought out my shop. The incubus is off—I can *live* now!"

He held his head up in a fine triumph, and she watched him adoringly.

"Did you—was it profitable?" she asked.

"It's all exchange, and some cash to boot. Just think! You know what I've wanted so long—a ranch. A big one that would keep us all, and let me go on with my work. And, dear—I've got it! It's a big fruit ranch, with its own water—think of that! And a vegetable garden, too, and small fruit, and everything. And, what's better, it's all in good running order, with a competent ranchman, and two Chinese who rent the vegetable part. And there are two houses on it—*two*. One for mother and the girls, and one for us!"

Diantha's heart stirred suddenly.

"Where is it, dear?" she whispered.

He laughed joyfully. "It's *here!*" he said. "About eight miles or so out, up by the mountains; has a little canyon of its own—its own little stream and reservoir. Oh, my darling! My darling!"

They sat in happy silence in the perfumed night. The strong arms were around her, the big shoulder to lean on, the dear voice to call her "little girl."

The year of separation vanished from their thoughts, and the long years of companionship opened bright and glorious before them.

"I came this afternoon," he said at length, "but I saw another man coming. He got here first. I thought—"

"Ross! You didn't! And you've left me to go without you all these hours!"

"He looked so confident when he went away that I was jealous," Ross admitted, "furiously jealous. And then your mother was here, and then those cackling girls. I wanted you—alone."

And then he had her, alone, for other quiet, happy moments. She was so glad of him. Her hold upon his hand, upon his coat, was tight.

"I don't know how I've lived without you," she said softly.

"Nor I," said he. "I haven't lived. It isn't life—without you. Well, dearest, it needn't be much longer. We closed the deal this afternoon. I came down here to see the place, and—incidentally—to see you!"

More silence.

"I shall turn over the store at once. It won't take long to move and settle; there's enough money over to do that. And the ranch pays, Diantha! It really *pays,* and will carry us all. How long will it take you to get out of this?"

"Get out of—what?" she faltered.

"Why, the whole abominable business you're so deep in here. Thank God, there's no shadow of need for it any more!"

The girl's face went white, but he could not see it. She would not believe him.

"Why, dear," she said, "if your ranch is as near as that it would be perfectly easy for me to come in to the business—with a car. I can afford a car soon."

"But I tell you there's no need any more," said he. "Don't you understand? This is a paying fruit ranch, with land rented to advantage, and a competent manager right there running it. It's simply changed owners. I'm the owner now! There's two or three thousand a year to be made on it—has been made on it! There is a home for my people—a home for us! Oh, my beloved girl! My darling! My own sweetheart! Surely you won't refuse me now!"

Diantha's head swam dizzily.

"Ross," she urged, "you don't understand! I've built up a good business here—a real successful business. Mother is in it; father's to come down; there is a big patronage; it grows. I can't give it up!"

"Not for me? Not when I can offer you a home at last? Not when I show you that there is no longer any need of your earning money?" he said hotly.

"But, dear—dear!" she protested. "It isn't for the money; it is the work I want to do—it is my work! You are so happy now that you can do your work—at last! This is mine!"

When he spoke again his voice was low and stern.

"Do you mean that you love—your work—better than you love me?"

"No! It isn't that! That's not fair!" cried the girl. "Do you love your work better than you love me? Of course not! You love both. So do I. Can't you see? Why should I have to give up anything?"

"You do not have to," he said patiently. "I cannot compel you to marry me. But now, when at last—after these awful years—I can really offer you a home—you refuse!"

"I have not refused," she said slowly.

His voice lightened again.

"Ah, dearest! And you will not! You will marry me?"

"I will marry you, Ross!"

"And when? When, dearest?"

"As soon as you are ready."

"But—can you drop this at once?"

"I shall not drop it."

Her voice was low, very low, but clear and steady.

He rose to his feet with a muffled exclamation, and walked the length of the piazza and back.

"Do you realize that you are saying no to me, Diantha?"

"You are mistaken, dear. I have said that I will marry you whenever you choose. But it is you who are saying, 'I will not marry a woman with a business.'"

"This is foolishness!" he said sharply. "No man—that is a man—would marry a woman and let her run a business."

"You are mistaken," she answered. "One of the finest men I ever knew has asked me to marry him—and keep on with my work!"

"Why didn't you take him up?"

"Because I didn't love him." She stopped, a sob in her voice, and he caught her in his arms again.

It was late indeed when he went away, walking swiftly, with a black rebellion in his heart; and Diantha dragged herself to bed.

She was stunned, deadened, exhausted; torn with a desire to run after him and give up—give up anything to hold his love. But something, partly reason and partly pride, kept saying within her: "I have not refused him; he has refused me!"

CHAPTER XIII: ALL THIS

They laid before her conquering feet
The spoils of many lands;
Their crowns shone red upon her head
Their scepters in her hands.

She heard two murmuring at night,
Where rose-sweet shadows rest;
And coveted the blossom red
He laid upon her breast.

When Madam Weatherstone shook the plentiful dust of Orchardina from her expensive shoes, and returned to adorn the more classic groves of Philadelphia, Mrs. Thaddler assumed to hold undisputed sway as a social leader.

The Social Leader she meant to be; and marshalled her forces to that end. She Patronized here, and Donated there; revised her visiting list with rigid exclusiveness; secured an Eminent Professor and a Noted Writer as visitors, and gave entertainments of almost Roman magnificence.

Her husband grew more and more restive under the rising tide of social exactions in dress and deportment; and spent more and more time behind his fast horses, or on the stock-ranch where he raised them. As a neighbor and fellow ranchman, he scraped acquaintance with Ross Warden, and was able to render him many small services in the process of settling.

Mrs. Warden remembered his visit to Jopalez, and it took her some time to rearrange him in her mind as a person of wealth and standing. Having so rearranged him, on sufficient evidence, she and her daughters became most friendly, and had hopes of establishing valuable acquaintance in the town. "It's not for myself I care," she would explain to Ross, every day in the week and more on Sundays, "but for the girls. In that dreadful Jopalez there was absolutely *no* opportunity for them; but here, with horses, there is no reason we should not have friends. You must consider your sisters, Ross! Do be more cordial to Mr. Thaddler."

But Ross could not at present be cordial to anybody. His unexpected good fortune, the freedom from hated cares, and chance to work out his mighty theories on the faithful guinea-pig, ought to have filled his soul with joy; but Diantha's cruel obstinacy had embittered his cup of joy. He could not break with her; she had not refused him, and it was difficult in cold blood to refuse her.

He had stayed away for two whole weeks, in which time the guinea-pigs nibbled at ease and Diantha's work would have suffered except for her mother's extra efforts. Then he went to see her again, miserable but stubborn, finding her also miserable and also stubborn. They argued till there was grave danger of an absolute break between them; then dropped the subject by mutual agreement, and spent evenings of unsatisfying effort to talk about other things.

Diantha and her mother called on Mrs. Warden, of course, admiring the glorious view, the sweet high air, and the embowered loveliness of the two ranch houses. Ross drew Diantha aside and showed her "theirs"—a lovely little wide-porched concrete cottage, with a red-tiled roof, and heavy masses of Gold of Ophir and Banksia roses.

He held her hand and drew her close to him.

He kissed her when they were safe inside, and murmured: "Come, darling—won't you come and be my wife?"

"I will, Ross—whenever you say—but—!" She would not agree to give up her work, and he flung away from her in reckless despair. Mrs. Warden and the girls returned the call as a matter of duty, but came no more; the mother saying that she could not take her daughters to a Servant Girls' Club.

And though the Servant Girls' Club was soon removed to its new quarters and Union House became a quiet, well-conducted hotel, still the two families saw but little of each other.

Mrs. Warden naturally took her son's side, and considered

Diantha an unnatural monster of hard-heartedness.

The matter sifted through to the ears of Mrs. Thaddler, who rejoiced in it, and called upon Mrs. Warden in her largest automobile. As a mother with four marriageable daughters, Mrs. Warden was delighted to accept and improve the acquaintance, but her aristocratic Southern soul was inwardly rebellious at the ancestorlessness and uncultured moneyed pride of her new friend.

"If only Madam Weatherstone had stayed!" she would complain to her daughters. "She had Family as well as Wealth."

"There's young Mrs. Weatherstone, mother—" suggested Dora.

"A nobody!" her mother replied. "She has the Weatherstone money, of course, but no Position; and what little she has she is losing by her low tastes. She goes about freely with Diantha Bell—her own housekeeper!"

"She's not her housekeeper now, mother—"

"Well, it's all the same! She *was!* And a mere general servant before that! And now to think that when Ross is willing to overlook it all and marry her, she won't give it up!"

They were all agreed on this point, unless perhaps that the youngest had her inward reservations. Dora had always liked Diantha better than had the others.

Young Mrs. Weatherstone stayed in her big empty house for a while, and as Mrs. Warden said, went about frequently with Diantha Bell. She liked Mrs. Bell, too—took her for long stimulating rides in her comfortable car, and insisted that first one and then the other of them should have a bit of vacation at her seashore home before the winter's work grew too heavy.

With Mrs. Bell she talked much of how Diantha had helped the town.

"She has no idea of the psychic effects, Mrs. Bell," said she. "She sees the business, and she has a great view of all it is going to do for women to come; but I don't think she realizes how much she is doing right now for women here—and men, too. There were my friends the Pornes; they were 'drifting apart,' as the novels have it—and no wonder. Isabel was absolutely no good as a housekeeper; he naturally didn't like it—and the baby made it all the worse; she pined for her work, you see, and couldn't get any time for it. Now they are as happy as can be— and it's just Diantha Bell's doings. The housework is off Isabel's shoulders.

"Then there are the Wagrams, and the Sheldons, and the Brinks—and ever so many more—who have told me themselves that they are far happier than they ever were before—and can live more cheaply. She ought to be the happiest girl alive!"

Mrs. Bell would agree to this, and quite swelled with happiness and pride; but Mrs. Weatherstone, watching narrowly, was not satisfied.

When she had Diantha with her she opened fire direct. "You ought to be the happiest, proudest, most triumphant woman in the world!" she said. "You're making oodles of money, your whole thing's going well, and look at your mother—she's made over!"

Diantha smiled and said she was happy; but her eyes would stray off to the very rim of the ocean; her mouth set in patient lines that were not in the least triumphant.

"Tell me about it, my friend," said her hostess. "Is it that he won't let you keep on with the business?"

Diantha nodded.

"And you won't give it up to marry him?"

"No," said Diantha. "No. Why should I? I'd marry him— to-morrow!" She held one hand with the other, tight, but they both shook a little. "I'd be glad to. But I will not give up my work!"

"You look thin," said Mrs. Weatherstone.

"Yes—"

"Do you sleep well?"

"No—not very."

"And I can see that you don't eat as you ought to. Hm! Are you going to break down?"

"No," said Diantha, "I am not going to break down. I am

doing what is right, and I shall go on. It's a little hard at first—having him so near. But I am young and strong and have a great deal to do—I shall do it."

And then Mrs. Weatherstone would tell her all she knew of the intense satisfaction of the people she served, and pleasant stories about the girls. She bought her books to read and such gleanings as she found in foreign magazines on the subject of organized house-service.

Not only so, but she supplied the Orchardina library with a special bibliography on the subject, and induced the new Woman's Club to take up a course of reading in it, so that there gradually filtered into the Orchardina mind a faint perception that this was not the freak of an eccentric individual, but part of an inevitable business development, going on in various ways in many nations.

As the winter drew on, Mrs. Weatherstone whisked away again, but kept a warm current of interest in Diantha's life by many letters.

Mr. Bell came down from Jopalez with outer reluctance but inner satisfaction. He had rented his place, and Susie had three babies now. Henderson, Jr., had no place for him, and to do housework for himself was no part of Mr. Bell's plan.

In Diantha's hotel he had a comfortable room next his wife's, and a capacious chair in the firelit hall in wet weather, or on the shaded piazza in dry. The excellent library was a resource to him; he found some congenial souls to talk with; and under the new stimulus succeeded at last in patenting a small device that really worked. With this, and his rent, he felt inclined to establish a "home of his own," and the soul of Mrs. Bell sank within her. Without allowing it to come to an issue between them, she kept the question open for endless discussion; and Mr. Bell lived on in great contentment under the impression that he was about to move at almost any time. To his friends and cronies he dilated with pride on his daughter's wonderful achievements.

"She's as good as a boy!" he would declare. "Women nowadays seem to do anything they want to!" And he rigidly paid his board bill with a flourish.

Meanwhile the impressive gatherings at Mrs. Thaddler's, and the humbler tea and card parties of Diantha's friends, had a new topic as a shuttlecock.

A New York company had bought one of the largest and finest blocks in town—the old Para place—and was developing it in a manner hitherto unseen. The big, shabby, neglected estate began to turn into such a fairyland as only southern lands can know. The old live-oaks were untouched; the towering eucalyptus trees remained in ragged majesty; but an army of workmen was busy under guidance of a master of beauty.

One large and lovely building rose, promptly dubbed a hotel by the unwilling neighbors; others, smaller, showed here and there among the trees; and then a rose-gray wall of concrete ran around the whole, high, tantalizing, with green boughs and sweet odors coming over it. Those who went in reported many buildings, and much activity. But, when the wall was done, and each gate said "No admittance except on business," then the work of genii was imagined, and there was none to contradict.

It was a School of Theosophy; it was a Christian Science College; it was a Free-Love Colony; it was a Secret Society; it was a thousand wonders.

"Lot of little houses and one big one," the employees said when questioned.

"Hotel and cottages," the employers said when questioned.

They made no secret of it, they were too busy; but the town was unsatisfied. Why a wall? What did any honest person want of a wall? Yet the wall cast a pleasant shadow; there were seats here and there between buttresses, and, as the swift California season advanced, roses and oleanders nodded over the top, and gave hints of beauty and richness more subtly stimulating than all the open glory of the low-hedged gardens near.

Diantha's soul was stirred with secret envy. Some big concern was about to carry out her dream, or part of it—

perhaps to be a huge and overflowing rival. Her own work grew meantime, and flourished as well as she could wish.

The food-delivery service was running to its full capacity; the girls got on very well under Mrs. Jessup, and were delighted to have a house of their own with the parlors and piazzas all to themselves, and a garden to sit in as well. If this depleted their ranks by marriage, it did not matter now, for there was a waiting list in training all the time.

Union House kept on evenly and profitably, and Diantha was beginning to feel safe and successful; but the years looked long before her.

She was always cheered by Mrs. Weatherstone's letters; and Mrs. Porne came to see her, and to compare notes over their friend's success. For Mrs. Weatherstone had been presented at Court—at more than one court, in fact; and Mrs. Weatherstone had been proposed to by a Duke—and had refused him! Orchardina well-nigh swooned when this was known.

She had been studying, investigating, had become known in scientific as well as social circles, and on her way back the strenuous upper layer of New York Society had also made much of her. Rumors grew of her exquisite costumes, of her unusual jewels, of her unique entertainments, of her popularity every-where she went.

Other proposals, of a magnificent nature, were reported, with more magnificent refusals; and Orchardina began to be very proud of young Mrs. Weatherstone and to wish she would come back.

She did at last, bringing an Italian Prince with her, and a Hoch Geborene German Count also, who alleged they were travelling to study the country, but who were reputed to have had a duel already on the beautiful widow's account.

All this was long-drawn gossip but bore some faint resem-blance to the facts. Viva Weatherstone at thirty was a very different woman front the pale, sad-eyed girl of four years earlier. And when the great house on the avenue was arrayed in new magnificence, and all Orchardina—that dared—had paid its respects to her, she opened the season, as it were, with a brilliant dinner, followed by a reception and ball.

All Orchardina came—so far as it had been invited. There was the Prince, sure enough—a pleasant, blue-eyed young man. And there was the Count, bearing visible evidence of duels a-plenty in earlier days. And there was Diantha Bell—receiving, with Mrs. Porne and Mrs. Weatherstone. All Orchardina stared. Diantha had been at the dinner—that was clear. And now she stood there in her soft, dark evening dress, the knot of golden acacias nestling against the black lace at her bosom, looking as fair and sweet as if she had never had a care in her life.

Her mother thought her the most beautiful thing she had ever seen; and her father, though somewhat critical, secretly thought so, too.

Mrs. Weatherstone cast many a loving look at the tall girl beside her in the intervals of "Delighted to see you's," and saw that her double burden had had no worse effect than to soften the lines of the mouth and give a hint of pathos to the clear depths of her eyes.

The foreign visitors were much interested in the young Amazon of Industry, as the Prince insisted on calling her; and even the German Count for a moment forgot his ancestors in her pleasant practical talk.

Mrs. Weatherstone had taken pains to call upon the Wardens—claiming a connection, if not a relationship, and to invite them all. And as the crowd grew bigger and bigger, Diantha saw Mrs. Warden at last approaching with her four daughters—and no one else. She greeted them politely and warmly; but Mrs. Weatherstone did more.

Holding them all in a little group beside her, she introduced her noble visitors to them; imparted the further information that their brother was *fiance* to Miss Bell. "I don't see him," she said, looking about. "He will come later, of course. Ah, Miss Madeline! How proud you all must feel of your sister-in-law to be!"

Madeline blushed and tried to say she was.

"Such a remarkable young lady!" said the Count to Adeline. "You will admire, envy, and imitate! Is it not so?"

"Your ladies of America have all things in your hands," said the Prince to Miss Cora. "To think that she has done so much, and is yet so young—and so beautiful!"

"I know you're all as proud as you can be," Mrs. Weatherstone continued to Dora. "You see, Diantha has been heard of abroad."

They all passed on presently, as others came; but Mrs. Warden's head was reeling. She wished she could by any means get at Ross, and *make* him come, which he had refused to do.

"I can't, mother," he had said. "You go—all of you. Take the girls. I'll call for you at twelve—but I won't go in."

Mr. and Mrs. Thaddler were there—but not happy. She was not, at least, and showed it; he was not until an idea struck him. He dodged softly out, and was soon flying off, at dangerous speed over the moon-white country roads.

He found Ross, dressed and ready, sulking blackly on his shadowy porch.

"Come and take a spin while you wait," said Mr. Thaddler.

"Thanks, I have to go in town later."

"I'll take you in town."

"Thank you, but I have to take the horses in and bring out my mother and the girls."

"I'll bring you all out in the car. Come on—it's a great night."

So Ross rather reluctantly came.

He sat back on the luxurious cushions, his arms folded sternly, his brows knit, and the stout gentleman at his side watched him shrewdly.

"How does the ranch go?" he asked.

"Very well, thank you, Mr. Thaddler."

"Them Chinks pay up promptly?"

"As prompt as the month comes round. Their rent is a very valuable part of the estate."

"Yes," Mr. Thaddler pursued. "They have a good steady market for their stuff. And the chicken man, too. Do you know who buys 'em?"

Ross did not. Did not greatly care, he intimated.

"I should think you'd be interested—you ought to—it's Diantha Bell."

Ross started, but said nothing.

"You see, I've taken a great interest in her proposition ever since she sprung it on us," Mr. Thaddler confided. "She's got the goods all right. But there was plenty against her here—you know what women are! And I made up my mind the supplies should be good and steady, anyhow. She had no trouble with her grocery orders; that was easy. Meat I couldn't handle—except indirectly—a little pressure, maybe, here and there." And he chuckled softly. "But this ranch I bought on purpose."

Ross turned as if he had been stung.

"You!" he said.

"Yes, me. Why not? It's a good property. I got it all fixed right, and then I bought your little upstate shop—lock, stock and barrel—and gave you this for it. A fair exchange is no robbery. Though it would be nice to have it all in the family, eh?"

Ross was silent for a few turbulent moments, revolving this far from pleasing information.

"What'd I do it for?" continued the unasked benefactor. "What do you *think* I did it for? So that brave, sweet little girl down here could have her heart's desire. She's established her business—she's proved her point—she's won the town—most of it; and there's nothing on earth to make her unhappy now but your pigheadedness! Young man, I tell you you're a plumb fool!"

One cannot throw one's host out of his own swift-flying car; nor is it wise to jump out one's self.

"Nothing on earth between you but your cussed pride!" Mr. Thaddler remorselessly went on. "This ranch is honestly yours—by a square deal. Your Jopalez business was worth the money—you ran it honestly and extended the trade. You'd have made a heap by it if you could have unbent a little. Gosh! I limbered up that store some in twelve months!" And the stout man smiled reminiscently.

Ross was still silent.

"And now you've got what you wanted—thanks to her, mind you, thanks to her!—and you ain't willing to let her have what she wants!"

The young man moistened his lips to speak.

"You ain't dependent on her in any sense—I don't mean that. You earned the place all right, and I don't doubt you'll make good, both in a business way and a scientific way, young man. But why in Hades you can't let her be happy, too, is more'n I can figure! Guess you get your notions from two generations back—and some!"

Ross began, stumblingly. "I did not know I was indebted to you, Mr. Thaddler."

"You're not, young man, you're not! I ran that shop of yours a year—built up the business and sold it for more than I paid for this. So you've no room for heroics—none at all. What I want you to realize is that you're breaking the heart of the finest woman I ever saw. You can't bend that girl—she'll never give up. A woman like that has got more things to do than just marry! But she's pining for you all the same.

"Here she is to-night, receiving with Mrs. Weatherstone— with those Bannerets, Dukes and Earls around her—standing up there like a Princess herself—and her eyes on the door all the time—and tears in 'em, I could swear—because you don't come!"

* * * *

They drew up with a fine curve before the carriage gate.

"I'll take 'em all home—they won't be ready for some time yet," said Mr. Thaddler. "And if you two would like this car I'll send for the other one."

Ross shook hands with him. "You are very kind, Mr. Thaddler," he said. "I am obliged to you. But I think we will walk."

Tall and impressive, looking more distinguished in a six-year-old evening suit than even the Hoch Geborene in his uniform, he came at last, and Diantha saw him the moment he entered; saw, too, a new light in his eyes.

He went straight to her. And Mrs. Weatherstone did not lay it up against him that he had but the briefest of words for his hostess.

"Will you come?" he said. "May I take you home—now?"

She went with him, without a word, and they walked slowly home, by far outlying paths, and long waits on rose-bowered seats they knew.

The moon filled all the world with tender light and the orange blossoms flooded the still air with sweetness.

"Dear," said he, "I have been a proud fool—I am yet—but I have come to see a little clearer. I do not approve of your work—I cannot approve of it—but will you forgive me for that and marry me? I cannot live any longer without you?"

"Of course I will," said Diantha.

CHAPTER XIV: AND HEAVEN BESIDE

They were married while the flowers were knee-deep over the sunny slopes and mesas, and the canyons gulfs of color and fragrance, and went for their first moon together to a far high mountain valley hidden among wooded peaks, with a clear lake for its central jewel.

A month of heaven; while wave on wave of perfect rest and world-forgetting oblivion rolled over both their hearts.

They swam together in the dawn-flushed lake, seeing the morning mists float up from the silver surface, breaking the still reflection of thick trees and rosy clouds, rejoicing in the level shafts of forest filtered sunlight. They played and ran like children, rejoiced over their picnic meals; lay flat among the crowding flowers and slept under the tender starlight.

"I don't see," said her lover, "but that my strenuous Amazon is just as much a woman as—as any woman!"

"Who ever said I wasn't?" quoth Diantha demurely.

A month of perfect happiness. It was so short it seemed but a moment; so long in its rich perfection that they both agreed if life brought no further joy this was Enough.

Then they came down from the mountains and began living.

* * * *

Day service is not so easily arranged on a ranch some miles from town. They tried it for a while, the new runabout car bringing out a girl in the morning early, and taking Diantha in to her office.

But motor cars are not infallible; and if it met with any accident there was delay at both ends, and more or less friction.

Then Diantha engaged a first-class Oriental gentleman, well recommended by the "vegetable Chinaman," on their own place. This was extremely satisfactory; he did the work well, and was in all ways reliable; but there arose in the town a current of malicious criticism and protest—that she "did not live up to her principles."

To this she paid no attention; her work was now too well planted, too increasingly prosperous to be weakened by small sneers.

Her mother, growing plumper now, thriving continuously in her new lines of work, kept the hotel under her immediate management, and did bookkeeping for the whole concern. New Union Home ran itself, and articles were written about it in magazines; so that here and there in other cities similar clubs were started, with varying success. The restaurant was increasingly popular; Diantha's cooks were highly skilled and handsomely paid, and from the cheap lunch to the expensive banquet they gave satisfaction.

But the "c. f. d." was the darling of her heart, and it prospered exceedingly. "There is no advertisement like a pleased customer," and her pleased customers grew in numbers and in enthusiasm. Family after family learned to prize the cleanliness and quiet, the odorlessness and flylessness of a home without a kitchen, and their questioning guests were converted by the excellent of the meals.

Critical women learned at last that a competent cook can really produce better food than an incompetent one; albeit without the sanctity of the home.

"Sanctity of your bootstraps!" protested one irascible gentleman. "Such talk is all nonsense! I don't want *sacred* meals—I want good ones—and I'm getting them, at last!"

"We don't brag about 'home brewing' any more," said another, "or 'home tailoring,' or 'home shoemaking.' Why all this talk about 'home cooking'?"

What pleased the men most was not only the good food, but its clock-work regularity; and not only the reduced bills but the increased health and happiness of their wives. Domestic bliss increased in Orchardina, and the doctors were more rigidly confined to the patronage of tourists.

Ross Warden did his best. Under the merciless friendliness of Mr. Thaddler he had been brought to see that Diantha had a right to do this if she would, and that he had no right to prevent her; but he did not like it any the better.

When she rolled away in her little car in the bright, sweet mornings, a light went out of the day for him. He wanted her there, in the home—his home—his wife—even when he was not in it himself. And in this particular case it was harder than for most men, because he was in the house a good deal, in his study, with no better company than a polite Chinaman some distance off.

It was by no means easy for Diantha, either. To leave him tugged at her heart-strings, as it did at his; and if he had to struggle with inherited feelings and acquired traditions, still more was she beset with an unexpected uprising of sentiments and desires she had never dreamed of feeling.

With marriage, love, happiness came an overwhelming instinct of service—personal service. She wanted to wait on him, loved to do it; regarded Wang Fu with positive jealousy when he brought in the coffee and Ross praised it. She had a sense of treason, of neglected duty, as she left the flower-crowned cottage, day by day.

But she left it, she plunged into her work, she schooled herself religiously.

"Shame on you!" she berated herself. "Now—*now* that you've got everything on earth—to weaken! You could stand unhappiness; can't you stand happiness?" And she strove with herself; and kept on with her work.

After all, the happiness was presently diluted by the pressure of this blank wall between them. She came home, eager, loving, delighted to be with him again. He received her with no complaint or criticism, but always an unspoken, perhaps imagined, sense of protest. She was full of loving enthusiasm about his work, and he would dilate upon his harassed guinea-pigs and their development with high satisfaction.

But he never could bring himself to ask about her labors with any genuine approval; she was keenly sensitive to his dislike for the subject, and so it was ignored between them, or treated by him in a vein of humor with which he strove to cover his real feeling.

When, before many months were over, the crowning triumph of her effort revealed itself, her joy and pride held this bitter drop—he did not sympathize—did not approve. Still, it was a great glory.

The New York Company announced the completion of their work and the *Hotel del las Casas* was opened to public inspection. "House of the Houses! That's a fine name!" said some disparagingly; but, at any rate, it seemed appropriate. The big estate was one rich garden, more picturesque, more dreamily beautiful, than the American commercial mind was usually able to compass, even when possessed of millions. The hotel of itself was a pleasure palace—wholly unostentatious, full of gaiety and charm, offering lovely chambers for guests and residents, and every opportunity for healthful amusement. There was the rare luxury of a big swimming-pool; there were billiard rooms, card rooms, reading rooms, lounging rooms and dancing rooms of satisfying extent.

Outside there were tennis-courts, badminton, roque, even croquet; and the wide roof was a garden of Babylon, a Court of the Stars, with views of purple mountains, fair, wide valley and far-flashing rim of sea. Around it, each in its own hedged garden, nestled "Las Casas"—the Houses—twenty in number, with winding shaded paths, groups of rare trees, a wilderness of flowers, between and about them. In one corner was a play-ground for children—a wall around this, that they might shout in freedom; and the nursery thereby gave every provision for the happiness and safety of the little ones.

The people poured along the winding walls, entered the pretty cottages, were much impressed by a little flock of well-floored tents in another corner, but came back with Ohs! and Ahs! of delight to the large building in the Avenue.

Diantha went all over the place, inch by inch, her eyes widening with admiration; Mr. and Mrs. Porne and Mrs. Weatherstone with her. She enjoyed the serene, well-planned beauty of the whole; approved heartily of the cottages, each one a little different, each charming in its quiet privacy, admired the plentiful arrangements for pleasure and gay association; but her professional soul blazed with enthusiasm over the great kitchens, clean as a hospital, glittering in glass and copper and cool tiling, with the swift, sure electric stove.

The fuel all went into a small, solidly built power house, and came out in light and heat and force for the whole square.

Diantha sighed in absolute appreciation.

"Fine, isn't it?" said Mr. Porne.

"How do you like the architecture?" asked Mrs. Porne.

"What do you think of my investment?" said Mrs. Weatherstone. Diantha stopped in her tracks and looked from one to the other of them.

"Fact. I control the stock—I'm president of the Hotel del las Casas Company. Our friends here have stock in it, too, and more that you don't know. We think it's going to be a paying concern. But if you can make it go, my dear, as I think you will, you can buy us all out and own the whole outfit!"

It took some time to explain all this, but the facts were visible enough.

"Nothing remarkable at all," said Mrs. Weatherstone. "Here's Astor with three big hotels on his hands—why shouldn't I have one to play with? And I've got to employ *somebody* to manage it!"

* * * *

Within a year of her marriage Diantha was at the head of this pleasing Centre of Housekeeping. She kept the hotel itself so that it was a joy to all its patrons; she kept the little houses homes of pure delight for those who were so fortunate as to hold them; and she kept up her "c. f. d." business till it grew so large she had to have quite a fleet of delivery wagons.

Orchardina basked and prospered; its citizens found their homes happier and less expensive than ever before, and its citizenesses began to wake up and to do things worth while.

* * * *

Two years, and there was a small Ross Warden born.

She loved it, nursed it, and ran her business at long range for some six months. But then she brought nurse and child to the hotel with her, placed them in the cool, airy nursery in the garden, and varied her busy day with still hours by herself—the baby in her arms.

Back they came together before supper, and found unbroken joy and peace in the quiet of home; but always in the background was the current of Ross' unspoken disapproval.

Three years, four years.

There were three babies now; Diantha was a splendid woman of thirty, handsome and strong, pre-eminently successful—and yet, there were times when she found it in her heart to envy the most ordinary people who loved and quarreled and made up in the little outlying ranch houses along the road; they had nothing between them, at least.

Meantime in the friendly opportunities of Orchardina society, added to by the unexampled possibilities of Las Casas (and they did not scorn this hotel nor Diantha's position in it), the three older Miss Wardens had married. Two of them preferred "the good old way," but one tried the "d. s." and the "c. f. d." and liked them well.

Dora amazed and displeased her family, as soon as she was of age, by frankly going over to Diantha's side and learning bookkeeping. She became an excellent accountant and bade fair to become an expert manager soon.

Ross had prospered in his work. It may be that the element of dissatisfaction in his married life spurred him on, while the unusual opportunities of his ranch allowed free effort. He had always held that the "non-transmissability of acquired traits" was not established by any number of curtailed mice or crop-eared rats. "A mutilation is not an acquired trait," he protested. "An acquired trait is one gained by exercise; it modifies the whole organism. It must have an effect on the race. We expect the sons of a line of soldiers to inherit their fathers' courage— perhaps his habit of obedience—but not his wooden leg."

To establish his views he selected from a fine family of guinea-pigs two pair; set the one, Pair A, in conditions of ordinary guinea-pig bliss, and subjected the other, Pair B, to a course of discipline. They were trained to run. They, and their descendants after them, pair following on pair; first with slow-turning wheels as in squirrel cages, the wheel inexorably going, machine-driven, and the luckless little gluttons having to move on, for gradually increasing periods of time, at gradually increasing speeds. Pair A and their progeny were sheltered and fed, but the rod was spared; Pair B were as the guests at "Muldoon's"—they had to exercise. With scientific patience and ingenuity, he devised mechanical surroundings which made them jump increasing spaces, which made them run always a little faster and a little farther; and he kept a record as carefully as if these little sheds were racing stables for a king.

Several centuries of guinea-pig time went by; generation

after generation of healthy guinea-pigs passed under his modifying hands; and after some five years he had in one small yard a fine group of the descendants of his gall-fed pair, and in another the offspring of the trained ones; nimble, swift, as different from the first as the razor-backed pig of the forest from the fatted porkers in the sty. He set them to race—the young untrained specimens of these distant cousins—and the hare ran away from the tortoise completely.

Great zoologists and biologists came to see him, studied, fingered, poked, and examined the records; argued and disbelieved—and saw them run.

"It is natural selection," they said. "It profited them to run."

"Not at all," said he. "They were fed and cared for alike, with no gain from running."

"It was artificial selection," they said. "You picked out the speediest for your training."

"Not at all," said he. "I took always any healthy pair from the trained parents and from the untrained ones—quite late in life, you understand, as guinea-pigs go."

Anyhow, there were the pigs; and he took little specialized piglets scarce weaned, and pitted them against piglets of the untrained lot—and they outran them in a race for "Mama." Wherefore Mr. Ross Warden found himself famous of a sudden; and all over the scientific world the Wiesmanian controversy raged anew. He was invited to deliver a lecture before some most learned societies abroad, and in several important centers at home, and went, rejoicing.

Diantha was glad for him from the bottom of her heart, and proud of him through and through. She thoroughly appreciated his sturdy opposition to such a weight of authority; his long patience, his careful, steady work. She was left in full swing with her big business, busy and successful, honored and liked by all the town—practically—and quite independent of the small fraction which still disapproved. Some people always will. She was happy, too, in her babies—very happy.

The Hotel del las Casas was a triumph.

Diantha owned it now, and Mrs. Weatherstone built others, in other places, at a large profit.

Mrs. Warden went to live with Cora in the town. Cora had more time to entertain her—as she was the one who profited by her sister-in-law's general services.

Diantha sat in friendly talk with Mrs. Weatherstone one quiet day, and admitted that she had no cause for complaint.

"And yet—?" said her friend.

Young Mrs. Warden smiled. "There's no keeping anything from you, is there? Yes—you're right. I'm not quite satisfied. I suppose I ought not to care—but you see, I love him so! I want him to *approve* of me!—not just put up with it, and bear it! I want him to *feel* with me—to care. It is awful to know that all this big life of mine is just a mistake to him—that he condemns it in his heart."

"But you knew this from the beginning, my dear, didn't you?"

"Yes—I knew it—but it is different now. You know when you are *married*—"

Mrs. Weatherstone looked far away through the wide window. "I do know," she said.

Diantha reached a strong hand to clasp her friend's. "I wish I could give it to you," she said. "You have done so much for me! So much! You have poured out your money like water!"

"My money! Well I like that!" said Mrs. Weatherstone. "I have taken my money out of five and seven per cent investments, and put it into ten per cent ones, that's all. Shall I never make you realize that I am a richer woman because of you, Diantha Bell Warden! So don't try to be grateful—I won't have it! Your work has *paid* remember—paid me as well as you; and lots of other folks beside. You know there are eighteen good imitations of Union House running now, in different cities, and three 'Las Casas!' all succeeding—and the papers are talking about the dangers of a Cooked Food Trust!"

They were friends old and tried, and happy in mutual affection. Diantha had many now, though none quite so dear. Her parents were contented—her brother and sister doing well—her children throve and grew and found Mama a joy they never had enough of.

Yet still in her heart of hearts she was not wholly happy.

* * * *

Then one night came by the last mail, a thick letter from Ross—thicker than usual. She opened it in her room alone, their room—to which they had come so joyously five years ago.

He told her of his journeying, his lectures, his controversies and triumphs; rather briefly—and then:

> My darling, I have learned something at last, on my travels, which will interest you, I fancy, more than the potential speed of all the guinea-pigs in the world, and its transmissability.
>
> From what I hear about you in foreign lands; from what I read about you wherever I go; and, even more, from what I see, as a visitor, in many families; I have at last begun to grasp the nature and importance of your work.
>
> As a man of science I must accept any truth when it is once clearly seen; and, though I've been a long time about it, I do see at last what brave, strong, valuable work you have been doing for the world. Doing it scientifically, too. Your figures are quoted, your records studied, your example followed. You have established certain truths in the business of living which are of importance to the race. As a student I recognize and appreciate your work. As man to man I'm proud of you—tremendously proud of you. As your husband! Ah! my love! I am coming back to you—coming soon, coming with my Whole Heart, Yours! Just wait, My Darling, till I get back to you!
>
> Your Lover and Husband.

Diantha held the letter close, with hands that shook a little. She kissed it—kissed it hard, over and over—not improving its appearance as a piece of polite correspondence.

Then she gave way to an overmastering burst of feeling,

and knelt down by the wide bed, burying her face there, the letter still held fast. It was a funny prayer, if any human ear had heard it.

"Thank you!" was all she said, with long, deep sobbing sighs between. "Thank you!—O—thank you!"